T0165542

Old Fashion

courage

VINCE ALBERTS

All the people in this story are fictitious
and so are the events that took place.

Order this book online at www.trafford.com
or email orders@trafford.com

Most Trafford titles are also available at major online book retailers.

Print information available on the last page.

ISBN: 978-1-4669-9044-9 (sc)
ISBN: 978-1-4669-9045-6 (e)

Because of the dynamic nature of the Internet, any web addresses or links contained in
this book may have changed since publication and may no longer be valid. The views
expressed in this work are solely those of the author and do not necessarily reflect the
views of the publisher, and the publisher hereby disclaims any responsibility for them.

Any people depicted in stock imagery provided by Thinkstock are models,
and such images are being used for illustrative purposes only.
Certain stock imagery © Thinkstock.

Trafford rev. 10/26/2015

 www.trafford.com

North America & international
toll-free: 1 888 232 4444 (USA & Canada)
fax: 812 355 4082

Preface

Cathy was never like all the other kids in her school, she was always a go getter and a hard worker. When the other kids were playing, she was working, they called her a workaholic. But she was always one step ahead of everyone else. She was that way from first grade right up to the twelfth grade. If there was ever anyone that deserved the best it was her. After she graduated from school she got a job and worked in a grocery store. But, what happened after that should never have happened.

Life can change, In a twinkling of an eye, and not always by your own hand. If It was, Her future would have been In hers. In this story, there Is a little fantasy, A tremendous amount of reality. And a whole bunch of emotions, and a lot of love. And the type of courage that is hard to believe.

Chapter 1

It was very dark on the street where she lived, the lighting was bad, very bad, lack of funds on the town's part no doubt. But Cathy walked that darkly lit street every night like clock work. Always at the same time and always the same route. And unbeknown to her she was being watched by someone every night. She was nineteen years old and worked very hard to get ahead and to make money for her family, she used to say. "I like this job, I think I'll stay here forever." She had worked at that corner store since she left high school and she kept advancing regularly because of her hard work and determination to get ahead, she had a bank account for the first time in her life and was saving money for her future.

After all, a girl has to watch out for her future, and she thought she would stay at that same job until it was time to make her decision as to what trade she was going to pursue, but not yet, she wasn't ready yet to plunge into some thing that she knew that she wasn't ready for. Until one night, as she was walking home, A figure jumped out of the shadows not far from her house and grabbed her. She struggled and tried to get free but her assailant hung on real tight, She managed to turn herself around while scratching and clawing and came up swiftly with her knee and caught him in a good spot.

But what she hadn't seen was the knife in his right hand, the assailant himself being in pain raised the knife and plunged it deep in her back. She let out a god awful scream and fell to the ground. A man who was across the street heard the young lady scream and ran towards where the screams were coming from and found her in a pool of blood. He turned back and yelled at his wife, "Call the police and get an ambulance." He knelt down beside her and felt her pulse to see if she was still alive, she was, he suddenly got a look of relief on his face and said.

"Lie still miss, help is on the way, he took a white handkerchief out of his pocket and placed it over the wound to try to slow down the bleeding. Just then he heard a siren, and looking up he saw a police car approaching, then from the distance he heard another, that of the ambulance. thinking, God, I hope she makes it, she's so young. The paramedics jumped out of the van and came over next to her and checked her very carefully, and one of them said. "That was quick thinking mister, you probably saved her life" One of them ran to the ambulance and came back with a stretcher, they picked her up very gently and placed her on the stretcher and put her in the ambulance and sped away. The following day, the man that had found her was driving by the hospital and thought he would stop and see how the girl was. When he approached the reception desk, he saw a big nurse at the desk that looked like she had put in two shifts in one and the mood she was in was anything but good, When he got to the desk he said.

"Excuse me, miss," the nurse said, "Yes, what can I do for you," he said, "There was a young lady brought in last night that was stabbed, and I was wondering if she was alright," she said, "And who are you?"

"My name is Fred Foster and I'm the man that found her last night and called the police."

She said, "Well, only family can go in to see her." Giving him a look that could start a forest fire. A man that was standing nearby, heard the conversation and came over to where Fred was standing and said.

"Excuse me, but I couldn't help overhearing what you said, are you the man that found my daughter.?"

"Yes sir." Fred said.

"I'm Cathy's father, and I want to thank you very much for what you did, the paramedics told me you tried to help her." "Yes sir I did." said Fred.

"Well, probably because of what you did, she is still hanging in there and we're hopeful that she will be okay."

Her father said.

looking at Fred with great admiration. The father said,

"Did you find out any more about what happened?"

"No, but the police are working on it." Fred said,

"I can't understand how one human can do that to another, If it's money or sex they want, why do they have to try to kill some one to get it?" said the father, Fred asked, "Yes I know." "Is she awake?" the Father answered, "No, she's in a coma." "Gees, that's too bad." he said with a real sad look on his face.

3

Fred asked the Father "Do you think she will be alright?" "It's too early to tell, her back is in pretty bad shape, and the doctors won't know until they take x-rays. Said the Father,

"I certainly hope she will be okay." Fred said The father's bottom lip started to tremble and a tear rolled out of his eye and he said.

"Yeah, me too." Then he turned to the nurse at the nursing station and said.

"Let this man go in to see my daughter any time he wants."

She said "I'm sorry sir, but only family can go in to see her." with an aggravated look on her tired face.

"He is family, he's my brother." the Father said

"If you say so sir." she said with a tone that she knew she had lost the battle. Fred said'

"Thanks, but you didn't have to do that."

"Yes I did, you saved my daughter's life." And at that point he threw his arms around him and said'

"Thank you. and by the way, my name is Del Woods and I'm very pleased to meet you, and I'm in the phone book, any time you want to call me and the Mrs. to check on Cathy, feel free."

"Thank you very much." Fred said.

It was true that Cathy's back was in very bad shape, the knife that was thrust in her back had cut a lot of tendons and the chords that control the legs and all the feeling for the lower extremities. And if she ever came out of the coma, she would never walk again.

Del pondered on all this and started crying, so young to have your life be over he murmured.

When Del got home, his wife wanted to know how she was and Del said. "Not good" "Have the doctors said anything?" she asked,

Del said "They don't think she will ever walk again." "Oh my god." said the Mother And she burst into tears. She asked, "Will she have to stay in the hospital long?" "That depends on how long she remains in a coma." Del said "Well I for one will be with her all day every day." the Mother answered.

"That's good honey." Del, now very exhausted said to his wife, "I'm gonna lay down for a while before supper If It's okay?" "That's fine babe." Cathy's mother Debbie, picked up the Phone and called her other daughter Brenda at work and filled her in on all that had happened and asked her If she was going to the hospital that night, Brenda, who loved Cathy very much said. "You bet I'm going, I want to give her all the support I can while she Is convalescing." "I'll pick you up after supper then." the Mother said.

That evening after supper they all got ready to go and when they got there, A Doctor Johnson met them in Cathy's room and asked If he could talk to Cathy's mom and dad.

Del noticed that this Doctor Johnson had a very worried look on his face and waited for the worse. He said,

"I'm Doctor Johnson, and I'll be doing the operation on your daughter Cathy, she showed some signs of coming out of her coma this morning." Debbie gasped, "But she hasn't come out yet, and we can't operate until she does, and even If she does come out now, we still can't operate because the wound is still too inflamed, so at this point, It's A waiting game." the Doctor said.

"I suppose that's all we can do. "Del said. "Doctor, our daughter was raised on love, and It's love that will see her through this." Debbie said.

"I certainly hope so cause she will need all the love she can get." the Doctor said.

They went back to the room and Debbie went over to her bed side and took Cathy's hand in hers and said.

"We're here honey," and she squeezed her hand, we'll help you through this." suddenly, she felt Cathy's hand squeeze a very tiny bit. her eyes opened wide and she told Del that Cathy had squeezed her hand a little bit and he said.

"It must have just been a muscle twinge or some thing."

Brenda said, "I'm telling you she squeezed my hand."

"Okay, maybe you're right," he said with a doubtful look on his face.

"Talk to her again." Del asked, so Debbie started to talk to her.

"Cathy, It's mommy honey, daddy and I are here for you and Brenda is here too, we'll stay with you all through this, You're in the hospital, but you will be fine." Then she felt Cathy squeeze her hand again and she started to cry and said. "Honey, she did It again, she squeezed my hand."

Del ran out of the room and went to the nurse`s station and asked them to page Dr. Johnson, and the nurse on duty picked up A microphone and started to page him. "Doctor

Johnson, room 324" "Doctor Johnson, room 324." and boy, It wasn't long, he was there. He came running in to the room and Debbie said'

"She squeezed my hand when I spoke to her."

"Can you talk to her again while I'm here?" the Doctor asked,

"Sure." So Debbie started to talk to her and the Doctor was watching, specifically her hands, after a couple of minutes she squeezed the mother's hand again. When the Doctor saw It, he freaked out.

"Keep talking to her, she's on her way out of her coma." he asked, Now, all three were talking to her Del, Debbie, and Brenda, talking to her like there was no tomorrow. Dr. Johnson said. "I have to get back to my rounds but you keep talking to her and If anything happens, call me." About two hours went by and the three family members were still pounding at her, and suddenly Cathy started to open her eyes. Del again ran out the door and to the nurse's station and ask the nurse one more time to call Doctor Johnson, and again she called him in the same fashion. A few minutes later he came running into the room and Cathy was looking at him and he said. Hi there young lady, I see you're back with us, you gave us quite a scare."

"What happened." she said. "You were attacked on the way home honey. "Debbie said. "Oh yes, I remember A little, Oh, my back hurts."

"I know honey, but Doctor Johnson Is here and he will take very good care of you." Debbie said,

"Now Cathy, besides your sore back, how do you feel?" asked the Doctor,

"Well, I feel like I lost part of me somewhere, Do you know what happened?" she asked, "Yes, you were attacked on your way home and you were stabbed in the back." she asked, "How bad Is It?" "Pretty bad, It did a considerable amount of damage, we will operate, but we have to take some x-rays and we also have to wait for the swelling to go down." the Doctor said, "You mean, I might not walk again?" Cathy said,

"That's right." he said, "Oh my God." she cried,

"Look, right now we don't know all that much, there's still a chance we might be able to do something." Dr. Johnson said, and Debbie said. "Now honey, don't imagine It worse then It Is, you know how Doctors are, they don't want to make a commitment. A tear rolled out of Cathy's eye and she said.

"God, what am I gonna do, Is my life over." Cathy cried, "Your life Is not over young lady." Del said. "But daddy, what If I can't walk?" she asked, "The Doctor said maybe, not definite."

"Plus It's not the end of the world, there Is still a lot we can do." Del said.

Well, the wound was healing good according to Doctor Johnson and the swelling had gone down so they took Cathy in for some x-rays so they could see the extent of the damage that was done.

Cathy came back from x-ray and Brenda was waiting for her, and Brenda thought that she was very pretty with a look of innocence of adolescence, but now there was a sadness in her eyes that ran deeper then life Itself.

A couple of days later, Doctor Johnson came in the room and said he wanted to talk to Cathy alone, or just her and her parents. After some of her friends left the room he started by saying.

"Cathy, we've gotten the x-rays back and have studied them very carefully and several Doctors and myself agree that there Is no need at this time to operate, because the damage Is too severe and It wouldn't benefit you."

"Oh my God mom, dad, I can't believe this, I'm only nineteen."

Cathy said, "Your well enough right now to go home If you so desire." Dr. Johnson said.

"Yes, I do." Cathy said "Okay then, I'll prepare the papers and you can go home today." Dr. Johnson said. By now the tears were flowing freely from all members of the family, Brenda came back In to the room and her mom took her out of the room again and told her. Brenda burst out crying and threw her arms around her mother's neck,

"Dear Lord mommy, how's she taking It?"

"Not too good, Debbie said, but she's coming home today and we'll help her all we can."

"We sure will." Brenda said,

Well, a few days went by and one day Del walked in the house after work and had a real nice wheel chair with him and he took It over to where Cathy was sitting and said,

"Look what I bought you today." Cathy said.

"I don't want It, I wont be rolling around In a wheel chair like an invalid." So Del just left It there. Even though she didn't want it at the time, her Father knew exactly what he was doing by leaving the chair by her. Del had big hopes for his daughter even though she wasn't in the mood for it he hoped she would be later.

Chapter 2

After supper Cathy wanted to use the phone to call one of her best friends and asked her dad If he would bring her the phone, Del said.

"The phone Is right there on the table honey, you've got wheels now you'll have to learn to use them."

"But daddy." she said very pitifully, But Del held his ground not wanting to show too much compassion because he knew that this had to be done. He turned his face away from her and you could see the pain he felt for his daughter. Debbie said.

"You're kinda hard on her aren't you?"

"Maybe, but I don't want her to be dependant on anyone, not even us." he said.

A few moments later Cathy really needed to use the phone, cause before her unfortunate accident, If you can call It that, she spent a lot of time on the phone like any teenager would. So she pulled the chair over to where she was sitting and with great difficulty at first she climbed Into It. Del heard her talking on the phone and he looked at Debbie with a grin on his face and making a gesture with his head like he had won. Debbie knew that It was best If Cathy learned to do things for herself because that was the kind of girl she was, although things were not the same now and never would be again.

The following morning Cathy got herself In her new set of wheels and rolled Into the kitchen for breakfast, she looked at Del and said.

"Like my new car daddy?" Cathy asked, A tear welled up In his eye and he said, he said, "Yes honey, I like your new car, It's a "Rolls" Isn't It?"

She said, "Yes, 1994 model with two hand power and palm breaks and all." Del said,

"After breakfast, why don't you take a stroll outside and get some fresh air."

She said, "Oh, I don't know If I'm ready for that yet, and besides, how would I go down the stairs?"

"Use the ramp." he said.

"What ramp?" she asked,

"The one I built In the garage last night." Del said,

"Oh, wise guy huh, Is there anything else you haven't told me." she asked, "Does Macy tell gimble ?" he said. "Yeah right daddy." she answered.

After breakfast Cathy went back Into the living room and puttered around with some of her things and she dozed off In her chair. Debbie came In the room and It woke her up and she said with a sleepy voice.

"Did dad have to get a chair that Is so comfortable?" she asked her Mother,

Debbie laughed and said. "You'll be fine honey and that makes me very happy." Cathy made It back to the kitchen and made herself a cup of coffee and placed a tray In her lap and put the coffee on It and went In to the living room again.

Debbie, seeing her do this said. "Hey, pretty soon you'll be able to go do the groceries." "Yeah right mom." she said with a grin. Debbie felt more pain then Cathy but she would never let It show In front of Cathy because she was afraid that Cathy would start to feel sorry for herself. Cathy placed her coffee on the small table In the entrance hallway where the phone was and started to make a call.

"Hello, Doctor Johnson, this Is Cathy Woods." "Yes Cathy, he said, what can I do for you?" "I want to talk to you about my back."

She asked, "Are you having problems?" and she said, "No, I want to talk to you about an operation." "Like I told you when you were here Cathy, there's nothing we can do." he said, "Well Doctor, I think there Is, and If you won't talk to me about It, I'll find some one who will." she said.

"But Cathy." but she hung up. Cathy had a small car that she had bought with some of the money she had saved up and luckily she thought, there were no payments on It but she sure couldn't drive It now.

She rolled over to the window and pushed the curtains aside and looked at It for a long time thinking how nice It would be If she could go for a ride. As she was looking out the window she saw a wine colored van pull up In the driveway and said to her mom.

"Hey mom, some one Is here."

She said, "I know honey." As she walked out of the bathroom. Cathy wondered how she knew, she couldn't have seen or heard the van come In the drive from the bathroom. Suddenly, Del walked In and said.

"Cathy, would you come out here please, your mom and I have something to show you."

"What have you gone and done daddy?" she asked,

"Not a thing, come on." he said, Cathy wheeled herself out to the back yard and there was the most beautiful van she had ever seen. "What Is this dad?" she asked, "It's your new van honey." he said, "What do you mean, my new van, I can't drive." she said, "Oh yes you can." he said, Del touched a button on the side door and the doors started to open very slowly and a ramp just seem to unfold from the side. Del said.

"Come over here, and roll yourself up on this ramp."

"You're kidding right?" she asked,

"Not at all sweety, come on." Del said,

So she started to roll her chair up on the ramp and It was a little hard at first but she managed to get It on there, then Del said. "Now, do you see that lever up over your head."

"Yeah." she said, "Pull down on It." he said, Cathy reached up and grabbed the lever and pulled down and the ramp started to move upwards, she said, "Whoa, this Is fun." After the ramp reached the top, It stopped and she said, "What do I do now."

"Roll your chair over to the steering wheel now and line yourself up under the wheel like you are going to drive." he said,

"Do you realize that most people drive four wheelers and I have six." she said, "Funny, funny." Del said. "Okay, now what, I still can't drive this thing." "Sure you can, now look, this Is the gas, this Is the break, this Is the shift, and this Is the signal lights." Del said.

"And you expect me to just jump In here and drive off Into the sunset." she said. "No, I expect you to come In here every day and familiarize yourself with all the controls." Del said. Sounding irritated.

"Okay, don't blow a gasket, I love you too." she said.

Del grinned and patted her on the head and said.

"It's all yours."

"Daddy, this van smells new." Cathy said,

"That's because It Is new." Del said.

"But, you can't afford this." she asked,

"Most of It was paid by the paraplegic foundation." he said.

Day after day she went In to the van and practiced with her new toy, she would have dry runs making believe that she was driving the van and looking In the rear view mirror and just getting used to It.

One day she thought she was ready to try this new machine that her dad had bought her so she got herself Into It and backed out of the yard. Del had told her that when she started to drive the van that she would have to go down and get a special license to drive it.

But for now, she was going down town, She was too determined at that point to worry about who was going to see her in the wheel chair. She parked the van on main street and got out and wheeled In to a small coffee shop, and lo and behold, who was there but, Doctor Johnson no less. Cathy got herself a cup of coffee and a donut and rolled over to where he was sitting and asked. "May I join you?" she asked "Oh yes, by all means Cathy, how are you?" he asked "I'm fine thank you." she said. "Are you still trying to find some one to operate on you?" he asked.

"Yes, I am, my dad Is buying me all sorts of medical Journals and I'm studying up for what I need." she said.

"Cathy, the best Doctors In the world couldn't repair the damage that was done by that knife." he said.

"I'm sorry Doctor, but I don't agree with you." she answered.

"That's your prerogative." he said.

"Yes I know, listen Doctor, A man cuts his finger off and he picks up the piece and runs to the hospital and they sew It back on, and you're telling me that they can't sew me back up?" she asked. "That's exactly what I'm telling you, It's not the same thing Cathy." he said. "It Is the same thing Doctor, It's just a matter of joining cables together, you go In and find the cables that make my legs work and you tie them back together." she said.

"Oh Cathy, If It were only as simple as you make It sound, don't you think I wouldn't have done It already." he replied.

"Doctor, when a wire breaks In your car you just get a connector and join both back together and It works, you can do the same thing with cables, or In this case tendons." she said.

"I know what you are saying but there has never been a procedure developed or Invented to repair an Injured back." he said.

"Then I will Invent one." she said, "I don't know how but I kinda hope you do." he said. "Well doctor, I'm sorry I took up all of your break time, and I will find a way." she said.

"I wish you all the luck In the world." Dr. Johnson said.

"You just don't know how bad I want to walk again." she said.

"Yes I know Cathy, but only God can perform miracles." he said. She finished her coffee and said, "see YA." and she rolled out of the restaurant leaving the Doctor still sitting there awed. Cathy got In her van and drove off, heading back home. When she got there, her mom came out of the house and said. "Honey, are you alright?" "Yes mom, why?" she asked. "Well I didn't notice when you left and I was worried." she said. "Oh, don't worry mom, I'm alright, I just went down town to have a coffee and I ended up having a coffee with Doctor Johnson."

"Doctor Johnson eh, and what did you two talk about?" she asked.

"My back, he still says It can't be done." she said. "Well, maybe he's right honey." Mom answered. "I don't think so, what he Is more then anything else Is unlearned." Cathy said. "Do you honestly think so?" Debbie asked.

"So much so that I can feel It In my bones." Cathy said.

Debbie helped her roll Into the house and she had lunch ready for her and Cathy said.

17

"I'm not too hungry mom, but It sure smells good, maybe I'll have a little with you." She had a bite and asked her mom If It would be okay If she laid down for a while. Debbie said. "Sure honey, I'll wake you up later for supper If you fall asleep." "Okay, thanks." Cathy said.

That night when she came to the supper table, she asked her dad If he'd had any luck In finding medical books or gotten any Information. Del said, he said. "Not much." That's when she thought of the library, she said. "I'll go down to the library tomorrow and see what I can find." Del asked. "Can you drive the van yet?" she said. "Oh yeah, I took It out today for a while." "Great, now we can take you down to get your license." Del said.

The next day she got up early and had breakfast and had a hopeful look on her face for once In a long time. The way she used to look every time something was happening in her life.

After breakfast she said so long to her mom, she didn't like goodbyes cause they were too final, and she got In her van and rode off. On the way down to the library she thought, I wonder If the library has a ramp? Aw they must have, a government building and all. Well when she rounded the corner she saw It, big as life, Its funny how when you don't use something you don't even realize that It's there. Anyway, she parked the van and disembarked and started to roll towards the ramp, when she got there she realized that the ramp was very steep and she stopped abruptly.

Chapter 3

And a man who was going In to the library saw her and he said. "Can I help you miss?" "If you wouldn't mind, It Is kinda steep." she said. So he gave her a push up the ramp and toward the front door. "Thank you." she said. "No problem miss, glad to be of service." he said back to her.

She thought, He's nice, I wonder If he's married, Yeah right Cathy, who would marry a cripple?.

when she went through the front door she activated an electric eye and the door opened all by Itself and she thought, WOW, I wish all the places had a gadget like that.

She rolled over to the front desk and asked the girl If they had any medical books, The girl said.

"All those are down stairs miss."

"And how do I get down there?" she asked.

"There's an elevator right over there and there's another girl down there that will take care of you." the lady said. Boy she thought, is this place organized or what. So off she went towards the elevator, she pushed the button and the doors opened and she rolled In, pushed basement and It started the decline. When the elevator stopped, she looked and there was another library In all It's glory, she wheeled over to the desk and asked the girl If they had any medical books? the lady said.

"What area of study are you Interested In?" "The back."

"Can you get the books down from the shelves for me?" she asked.

The lady said, "This floor Is built specially for wheel chairs, go down isle M and all the books that you are looking for are at your finger tips.

"Gees, That's great thanks." "No problem miss." Cathy said.

She went to isle M and turned In and there In front of her were all the medical books ever written. She searched all morning and couldn't find anything, the girl at the desk had given her a special table that hooked to her chair so she could set the book down and read It. After a while the girl came over to check on her to make sure she was alright. Cathy said. "I haven't found anything, can I come back after lunch?" Cathy said, "Sure, no problem." the lady said.

Then Cathy said. "Great, I'll be back." And she headed for the elevator.

Well, Cathy found out that It wasn't gonna be that easy, she went back day after day and wasn't finding anything, Oh she studied and made notes but nothing concrete. One day though, she picked up a book by a Doctor James Franklin, she looked at It and sort of groaned as she read on.

The book was specifically about back problems, but the book was published In 1911 and It was now 1994. Could It be possible that this Doctor Franklin would still be alive.

She went over to the desk and asked the girl If It would be possible for her to check the book out of the library, the girl said' "Sure, just fill out this card and show me some I.d. and the book Is yours for one month, and please be careful with that book, It's a one of a kind." "I'll guard it with my life" Cathy filled out the form rolled herself back to her van and drove home.

All at once a car pulled out In front of her and she had to slam on the breaks to keep from hitting It. she thought, that's all I need, an accident, I had better calm down and slow down If I want to make It home, thinking that she might have been a bit excited because of what she had found, maybe she wasn't as alert as she could have been.

Cathy was very tired from her ordeal and when she got home she put the book on the night stand and drifted off to sleep. she didn't hear Debbie as she came In to check on her.

The next morning she woke up early and had coffee with her dad and told him about the book she had found, and Del said. "Honey, why are you doing this to yourself? you know what the Doctors said, there Is nothing anyone can do."

"Oh daddy, don't you side In with them, It's hard enough doing this, I don't need you against me too." she stammered.

"I'm not against you honey, I'm just facing facts, If they could do something don't you think they would have done It by now." Del said. I have a book here that says that It can be done." Cathy said. "Let me see that book." Del said. "It's a book that was written by a Doctor James Franklin." Cathy said

"This book was published In 1911, the Doctor can't possibly be still alive." Del said. "I don't know, but I'm gonna try to find out." Cathy said. "I admire your courage sweetheart but I have to get to work." Del said. Del left for work and she thought of calling Doctor Johnson but she knew that he wouldn't be In his office till 10:00 A.M.

So she settled back In her wheelchair and started to read In Doctor Franklin's book.

According to Doctor Franklin, the procedure Is a fairly simple one, but It takes a long time to tie all the chords together with something he calls fusion, what ever that Is.

Around 9:30 she got dressed and rolled out to her van and headed down town.

The ride to the Doctor's office wasn't very long, but for Cathy It seemed like forever, because handling all those controls by hand was a big chore. She got to the Doctor's office and the secretary said that he wasn't In yet and that she would have to wait.

A half hour went by and he still wasn't In so she told the lady that she was going for coffee and that she would return and she left. She went downstairs to the coffee shop and ordered some breakfast and some coffee and went to a table to eat, a young man that worked there brought her food to the table and said. "Enjoy your breakfast." As If moved by providence, a man came over and asked If he could sit with her because there was no where else to sit. Cathy said.

"Sure, no problem." he sat down and started a conversation by saying, "Are you here to see a Doctor?"

"Yes, Doctor Johnson." Cathy said, "I'm a Doctor In this building also." He said. "Oh are you? Cathy replied, what's your name?" she asked, "Doctor West." he said.

"Are you a general practitioner?" she asked. "No, I'm a Gynaecologist." he said.

"Well, I don't need one of those, I need a Doctor for my back."

She said. "What's the problem?" he asked.

"I got stabbed In the back and I need some one to repair the damage." she said,

"I don't think that procedure can be done." he said.

"Yes It can, have you ever heard of a Doctor James Franklin?" she asked. "Yes, years ago, but he's dead now." he said. "Do you know that for sure?" she asked "Yes." "Well, when he was alive, he performed the operation more then once according to his book."

"Well, I hate to burst your bubble but the man was a quack." he said. "He might have been a quack In your eyes, but If what he says Is true, he's a saint In mine." she said.

"Well, I must be off to work, good luck." he said. "Thanks, bye." she said.

Cathy finished her coffee and headed back upstairs to see Doctor Johnson, when she walked In he was standing In the waiting room, he turned and saw her and said.

"Cathy, come on In right now so you won't have to wait around too long. She went In and started to tell him about this

Doctor James Franklin, and he looked at her very strangely and said.

"All I know about him Is what I've heard and that was that he was a quack and he didn't know what he was talking about." he said.

"According to this book, he did know what he was talking about, did you ever stop and think that maybe he was ahead of his time and It was everyone else that was wrong." she asked.

"I'll make a deal with you Cathy, If you find me one person that he performed the operation on successfully, I'll read the book." Dr. Johnson said. "You`ve got yourself a deal." Cathy said.

Cathy left and drove back home thinking, now I've gone and done It, and my work Is just beginning. That night, she talked to her dad when he got home from work and told him what she was planning to do. And he said. "Honey, why are you pursuing this, when you know It's futile." Big tears came to Cathy's eyes and she said to her dad, "Daddy, not meaning any disrespect, but It's not you that's stuck to a wheel chair, It's me, and I'm fighting for my life here, and I may need your help from time to time, Is that too much to ask." by now Del and Debbie both were crying and Del said. "I'm sorry honey," rubbing his eyes, "I guess I wasn't thinking of you, just the problem." "I know that It's my problem and I have to deal with It, and that is what I'm trying to do." Cathy cried. by then she was crying full blast.

"Honey, I'm really sorry, I've been very Insensitive to your situation." Del said. "That's okay daddy, I get It from everybody." Cathy said.

"Well, you won't get It from me any more, what can I do to help you." Del asked. "I don't know daddy, I just don't know where to start." Cathy said.

"Well, why don't you start with what you would like to do and we'll start there." her Father said.

she told him about her visit with Doctor Johnson and what he had said and what she felt she had to do. "Okay, what can I do." Del asked. Cathy asked, "You said you were off next week?" Cathy asked. "Yes I am." Del said. "Come with me and help me track down some of the people that he cured." she said.

"I'm ready, where do we start?" Del said. "Thanks daddy, but that's just It, I don't know where to start." Cathy said.

"Let me see that book again." Del asked.

Del took the book and read in it for a long time and then he said.

"Listen, one of the people he cured lived In Janeville, why don't we start there?" Del asked.

"Well we could I suppose, what do we have to lose." Cathy said. The weekend was a long time coming and Cathy wasn't used to waiting around that way, she was too much of a live wire to just be sitting around.

That part of her hadn't changed she thought, and If she didn't get her legs back she would have to get a job working with her head.

Saturday morning she decided to drive down to the local coffee shop and have a cup cause she used to meet all her friends there, but she hadn't been there since her accident and she didn't know how her friends were going to react.

She parked the van and went in and a girl she knew came over and opened the door for her and as soon as she rolled inside the place, everybody got up and started to sing, for she's a jolly good fellow. Again she got tears in her eyes and was almost crying, It made her feel good but In a sad kinda way, she said hello to everyone except the boy she was sweet on, he wasn't there that day. Everyone wanted to know what had happened and she said' "Its not a very pleasant thing and If It's all the same to you guys, I'd rather not talk about It. Cathy said. Everybody said fine, If she didn't feel like talking about It, that was okay. They all agreed that It wouldn't hurt their friendship. She did tell a few close friends about her plans to try to find some people that were cured by this Doctor Franklin, and every one wished her luck. One of her girlfriends said. "I admire your courage girl, you've got a lot of moxie." "After all, I still want to enter that dance contest with you guys." Cathy said. The girls all laughed and went on to catch up on all the gossip. Hey, a girl has to be In touch right.

She managed to kill a lot of time with her friends and when she looked at her watch.

It was passing lunch time and she said she had to go home, the girls all wanted her to have lunch with them and she said that she had to go home first because she had wheelchair facilities at home. One girl said. "Grady Installed some of those in the lady's room just last week because of you Cathy."

"You're kidding right?" Cathy asked. "No not at all, come on we'll show you." the girl said. Cathy was glad In a way cause lunch with these girls was an experience that no one should miss. After lunch she drove back home feeling much better, they had a way of making you feel good about yourself no matter who you were or what you were.

When she got home, her dad handed her a small hand held phone and said. "Would you please carry this with you at all times so we can find you." "Were you looking for me?" Cathy asked.

"Yes and no." Del said "but we were worried, cause we didn't know where you were." "When I used to disappear on you before, where did you usually find me?" Cathy asked. "At the coffee shop." her mom said. "Oh, now why didn't I think of that." Del said with a slight grin on his face but you could tell, It still bothered him not knowing where she was.

Chapter 4

Finally, Monday morning rolled around and Cathy and her dad were ready to take off for Janeville so they got In to Cathy's van and left.

"There's only one problem that I can see, I can't drive your van so you will have to do the driving and I will do the leg work." Del said.

"If you do that, I want you to be persevering, don't take no for an answer." Cathy said.

"Okay honey, I'll try." Del replied.

"It's about an hour to Janesville so when we get there we'll stop and have a coffee before we start looking." Cathy said.

"Sounds good." Del said.

"Lets hope that Janesville believes In wheel chair ramps." Cathy said.

Del said. "Yeah, otherwise you'll have to stay In the van all the time."

Cathy was right, It took about an hour to get to Janesville and when they got there Del found a real nice coffee shop and they went In and relaxed for a while. Del asked the shop owner If he knew of a Francis Boutier In Janesville, he said he didn't know him, and Del said.

"It's a her."

"No, I've never heard of her, but If she used to live In Janesville why don't you try the hospital?" the man said.

"Thank you, That's a good Idea, we'll do that." "Are you about done honey?" Del asked. "Yeah dad, lets go." Cathy said.

Del got directions from the owner on how to get to the hospital and he told him, so Del paid the bill and they left. Up one street and down another and finally they saw the hospital and pulled In to the parking lot, Del said.

"Why don't you wait here and I'll check It out." "Okay dad." Cathy said. A few minutes went by and Del came back and said.

"They said she used to live here a long time ago but she moved to Forest View, that's a small town about fifty miles from here, that was some time back and they lost track of her after that." "Lets follow It up." Cathy said.

"Okay, let's go." Del said. They drove about an hour and they came on to a quaint place on the right side of the road and kinda set back In a grove of pines and Del said.

"What do you say we have lunch here?"

"Looks good, look how clean the grounds are daddy."

"If the Inside Is as clean, we'll enjoy our food." Del said.

Cathy pulled In to the drive and parked the van and asked,

"How much farther do you figure It Is to Forest View?"

"Oh probably about twenty minutes." Del said.

They went In and the place was chuck full of old tables and chairs and stuff and Del said.

"There's a bloody fortune In antiques In here."

"Yes, so I see." Cathy said.

They found a table In the corner of the room so they could have a little privacy and the waitress came over to take their order.

"What will you have?" she asked.

"Oh I don't know, we'd like to relax for a few minutes, just bring us a coffee and the menu and we'll order later." Del said.

"Okay." she said and she went back Into the kitchen. A few minutes later she came over and set the table with place mats and glasses of water and she said.

"Just call me when you are ready."

"Okay." Del said. They talked for a few minutes just for conversation's sake and Del motioned to the waitress to come and take their order. Del ordered for both of them and he said.

"Pass me the phone for a minute, I want to call your mother so she won't worry."

"Will that reach home from here?" Cathy asked.

"It had better." He dialed the number and he said.

"Hello, we're just outside Forest View and we're having lunch, we should be home around supper time, you know the number If you need to call for anything honey, okay, bye."

"You told mom we'd be home by supper time, you think we will?" Cathy asked.

"Oh yeah, we should." Del said.

They had a very good lunch and afterwards Cathy Insisted on paying for the food and Del said.

"You're paying for the gas, I will pay for the food."

"Oh daddy." Cathy said. They left the restaurant and drove to Forestview, when they got there they decided to go directly to the hospital and check on the lady they were looking for. Cathy parked the van and Del went in to talk to some one about this woman, He walked in and went over to the receptionist and asked her.

"Excuse me miss but have you ever heard of a Francis Boutier In Forest View?"

"No sir, I can't say I have, but maybe Mabel would, she's the oldest nurse here." the lady said.

"And where can I find her?" Del asked.

"Right up those stairs and second door to your right." she said.

"Thank you." Del replied.

Del went up the stairs and knocked on the door that the nurse had told him to and a woman said.

"Come in." Del walked In and there sat an old nurse that looked over her glasses at him and said.

"Yes?"

"Hi, my name Is Del Woods and I'm looking for a woman that someone told me moved to this town a few years ago, her name Is Francis Boutier.

"Seems to me I've heard that name before, let me check my files and see what I can find, what do you want her for?" she asked.

"She was suppose to have had an operation by a Doctor James Franklin and we wanted to talk to her about It." Del said.

"Yes, here we are, Oh, according to this she passed away last year." the lady said.

"Did she leave any relatives behind?" Del asked.

"Don't know, you'd have to go to the newspaper office for that, maybe they could tell you." she said.

"And where do I find the newspaper office?" Del asked.

"Go out the driveway and turn left and go down two blocks and It'll be on your left." she said.

"Thank you." Del returned,

"You're welcome." she replied.

Del went back out to the van and told Cathy what had happened and they drove off down the street towards the newspaper office, when they got there, Cathy said.

"They have a ramp, I'm coming in with you."

"You need a hand?" Del asked.

"No, I'm fine, I got the hang of this a while back." Cathy said.

They went in to the office and there was a heavy man sitting at a desk and he looked up and said.

"Yes, can I help you?"

"Well, we're looking for some relatives that a Francis Boutier might have left when she passed away." Del asked.

"Boutier was her maiden name, she was my mother." the man said.

"Oh really, we'd like to ask you some questions about her." Del said.

"What kind of questions?" he asked.

"Well, she was supposed to have had an operation on her back performed by a Doctor James Franklin, Do you know anything about that?" Del asked.

"I don't rightly recollect and I don't remember that Doctor either, and I don't rightly know who could tell you about it, maybe Martha." He said.

He picked up the phone and called someone and said.

"Did mom ever have an operation on her back by a Doctor James Franklin,? yeah yeah, okay, but how are they going to find her,? okay, I'll tell em, bye, that was my older sister martha and she don't rightly remember, but she says that Dr. Franklin's grand daughter lives over in Jasper Ville and she has boasted that she has all of her grandfather's records." the man said.

"What's her name?" Del asked.

"Alice Bains." he said.

"Thank you very much." Del replied.

Del and Cathy left and Del said.

"Honey, we had better head for home and we'll attack that one tomorrow, what do you say?"

"Well, Jasper Is quite far so maybe you're right." Cathy said.

"Hey, looking at the map here, It looks like Jasper Is closer from home then from here anyway." Cathy said.

"Tomorrow Is another day honey, we won't give up." Del said.

"Thanks daddy." Cathy replied.

"How's the gas In here?" Del asked.

"Fine, we've only used a quarter of a tank so far." Cathy said.

"Wow, this thing Is pretty good on gas." Del said.

Cathy turned the van around and headed for home, "I'm glad you agreed to pay for the food instead of the gas." Cathy said. they both laughed. When they got back home they sat down and had a good cup of coffee and told Debbie everything that had happened. Cathy said.

"Mom, you don't mind that daddy and I are doing this do you?"

"No honey, not at all, In fact, tomorrow I'm going with you." Debbie said.

"All right, great stuff, I love you mom." Cathy said.

"I love you too honey." Debbie replied.

That night, Cathy pondered on what had happened and what she thought her chances were of proving that Dr. Franklin wasn't a quack, and If he was not, It will still be a hard job to get someone to operate because It's not standard procedure. The next morning It was raining and when Cathy got up she said.

"Well, there goes today, I don't like to drive In the rain cause I can't see as good and It scares me."

"We'll use my car." Del said.

"I don't know dad, It's raining so hard." Cathy said.

"It'll be fine honey, after all, we have to find that woman don't we." Del said.

"I'd like to." Cathy replied.

"Well then, let's do It." Del said.

On the way to Jasper Ville, the rain stopped and the sun started to shine and It looked like It was gonna be a beautiful day. The trip from Deluth to Jasper Ville usually took about two hours and after driving for a while, Del pulled in to a road side Inn and went in to get some coffee and donuts and they ate In the car. Debbie had fallen asleep In the back seat, afterwards, the girls went to the bathroom and they resumed the trip. When they finally got to Jasper, Del said to Cathy,

"We've had good luck with newspaper people, what do you say we start there."

"Sure, It's okay with me." Cathy said.

When they arrived at the paper, Cathy looked and said.

"Hey, I see they have a ramp, can you get my chair out of the trunk daddy?" "Sure thing miss." Del jokingly said.

"Cute daddy." Cathy said.

They got Inside and Cathy rolled over to the desk and asked,

Chapter 5

"**E**xcuse me, we are trying to find a woman that lives In Jasper Ville, her name Is Alice Bains." Oh yeah, that's old pinhead's daughter, George Franklin the Inventor.

That man Invented more garbage that didn't work just like his father before him, always coming up with new Idea's that didn't work." The man said.

"I would still like to talk to her." said Cathy.

He said. "Well, just go straight down this here road and you'll come to a fork In the road, go right and It's the fourth house on the left."

Cathy said. "Thank you." And back In the car they went and down the road to the house that the man had told them about only to find that the house had burned to the ground. Cathy said.

"Oh my God, maybe If we ask some of the neighbors and ask them what happened."

"I have to give you credit, you don't give up." Del said.

"I will never give up daddy." Cathy's reply.

They drove over to the only neighbor that they could see and asked what had happened to the house that had burned down. The people didn't know too much about It. Cathy asked.

"Was there anybody living In the house when It burned?"

"No Mam, I don't think so, the lady that was living there moved out some time before the house burned, the fire was a result of some kids playing with matches."

"Do you have any Idea where the lady moved to?" asked Cathy.

"Yeah, somebody said that she moved over to castle hill last year and we've not seen her since." the person said.

"Thank you very much." Del said.

"Hey you guy's what do you say we get some lunch and we'll discuss the whole thing then."

"Okay, I guess so." Cathy said.

So off they went again to another restaurant to have lunch. As they were sitting there Cathy asked.

"Where Is castle hill?"

"I don't know, but I can find out." Del said.

The waiter came over and asked them If they wanted the special or would they like to pick something from the menu. Del said.

"just bring the menu and we will decide later, By the way, do you know where castle hill Is?"

"Yeah, about ten miles up that mountain road." he said. As he pointed out the window towards the mountain.

"Thank you very much." Del said. They had a real good lunch and then started the ride up the mountain to try to find Alice Bains, up the winding climbing road and It looked like It wasn't going to stop climbing. But after a long while they started to see some houses and stores and pretty soon they saw a sign that read, entering Castle Hill. Del said.

"I don't imagine that there's a newspaper office In this burg."

"Stop at that gas station daddy." Cathy said.

"Okay." Del replied.

The attendant came out and came over to the car and asked,

"Can I help you folks?"

"Maybe, would you happen to know an Alice Bains?" asked Del.

"Yeah, she's the librarian, turn left right there and it's the big red building on your left." he said.

"Thank you." Cathy said.

So Del turned where the guy said and there It was, the big building, just like he said.

"I'm coming with you daddy." Cathy said.

"Okay honey." Del said. "I've come too far to quit now." she said.

So they all went In to the library and at the desk was a small woman In a drab gray dress and glasses hanging on her nose like they were going to fall off any minute, Cathy studied her for a second and said.

"Excuse me, are you Alice Bains?"

The woman said, "Yes."

"Whew, we've been looking all over for you." Cathy said.

"Well you've found me, what can I do for you?" she asked.

"Are you Doctor James Franklin's grand daughter?" Cathy asked.

"Yes again, what's this all about?" she asked.

"I understand you still have all of your grandfather's records?" Cathy asked.

"I have most of them, would you mind telling me what this Is all about?" she asked. "Your grandfather had developed a way to rejoin back muscles and nerves and tendons and had performed the procedure successfully on more then one person." Cathy said. "Yes, but no one believed him." she said. "Well I do." Cathy said. "It's kinda late now, he's dead." she answered. "It's never too late to give Dr. Franklin the recognition he deserves." Cathy said. "But I don't understand, what can I do?" she said. "Do you have the names of the ones he cured?" Cathy asked. "Oh yes." she said.

Cathy's heart leaped Inside of her and she got big tears In her eyes and she cried.

"Daddy." Cathy cried.

"Easy girl, don't fall apart on me now." Del said

"Alice, I've come a long way and I've waited a long time, Is there any way we could see those records?" Cathy asked. "Sure, If you want to." she said. "Your precious, when?" Cathy asked. "Now." she said. "You have the records here?" Cathy asked. "No, but, I'll get Gerty to cover for me for a minute and I'll go get them, I just live across the street." she said. "Great." Cathy replied.

Cathy looked like she was going to faint and her mother had to sit with her and console her. A few minutes went by and Alice came In with an old folder that looked like If you tried to open It, It would crack, and she said.

"All of my grandfather's records wouldn't help you but this folder has the names of all the people he operated on for severed back muscles." she said. "How many did he do?" asked Cathy. "Seven." she said. "All successful?" Cathy asked. "Yes." she said "You see, gramps was getting old and he did these before he died, all of them were volunteers for the operation." she said. "Are any of them still alive?" Cathy asked.

"I don't know, but what you can do though Is take down all the names and addresses and see If you can find them." Alice said

"If we can have the names, that's good enough for me." Cathy said.

"Baby, don't build up your hopes too high." "Hope Is all I have mom." Cathy said, "Well, what are we waiting for." Del said.

They copied down all the names that were on the list and asked Alice for her address and phone number so they could let her know what was going on. Alice said.

"I'd like that, and good luck." Alice said. "Thank you very much, you may have given me my legs back." Cathy said. "I know If gramps was here you'd get em back, that I know." Alice said. "Oh, by the way, do you have all of your grandfather's notes on the procedure for the operation?"

Cathy asked. "Oh yeah." Alice said. "That's fantastic, I'll be in touch, Bye." Cathy had never felt such elation, she said, "dad, I'm on cloud nine". "I can see that". he answered.

Well, the ride home was anything but quite, Cathy was talking a mile a minute and Debbie was speculating on the possibilities of the Information they had gotten. Debbie said.

"Cathy, at first like your father I believed the Doctors, but you have made a believer out of me and I'm with you 100 per cent."

"Thanks mom, I needed to hear you say that, thanks." Cathy said.

"Dad, what are we gonna do if we can't find any of the people on the list?" Cathy asked.

"Well In that case we have an ace In the hole don't we?" he said.

"What do you mean?" Cathy asked.

"Alice, she has the procedural notes doesn't she?" Del asked.

"Yes she does." Cathy said.

"Well, we can start there, although we would have to have a Doctor that would want to take on the A.M.A, of course, back then I don't think there was an American Medical Association, It would be Interesting to look Into." Del said. "Well, I think we will go home and rest for a day cause everybody Is pretty tired." Del said.

"I know I am." said Cathy.

"Well." Debbie said, "I'm with you all the way and when you're ready to go, so am I." Every one was glad to get home after the trip, Cathy found the car much less comfortable then the van, her chair was unbelievingly comfortable. She said to her mom and dad,

"I'm gonna lay down for a while, mom, why don't we send out for some pizza or something, you must be tired too."

"Okay honey, and the pizza sounds good." Del said.

"Yes, It sure does." Debbie said.

After a good night's rest, Cathy got up about 11:00 AM and had a good breakfast and told her dad that she was going down town to gas up her van to get ready for the next day.

So she wheel herself out of the house and got In her van, even the predicament she was In, she enjoyed riding up the ramp to get In her van. And she thought, I must still be a big baby cause I have fun doing that. She locked her chair In place and started the motor, she purred like a kitten, and she backed out of the drive. She thought, I'm still pretty Independent even though I can't walk. At the gas station she saw a young man that she was sweet on at one time, before her accident and she asked him If he would like to go for a malt or something so they could talk and he said,

"Gee no, I have to go right home cause my mom Is waiting for me." Cathy said.

"Okay." and drove off.

She was such In the habit of stopping for coffee here and there that she automatically pulled In to a drive In and wheeled herself In. She found a table and ordered a coffee and asked the waitress If she had any Danish pastries, and the waitress said.

42

"Yes."

"Could you bring me one please." Cathy asked.

"Sure, coffee?" the waitress said.

"Yes please with cream." Cathy replied.

"Very good, I'll be right back." the waitress said.

Chapter 6

She was thinking how strangely Bobby acted at the gas station when she heard a voice.

"Cathy?"

"Yes." she answered.

"Hi, I'm sorry If I Ignored you back there at the gas station, but, you know how It Is." he said.

"Yes I do Bobby, and you really are sorry, In fact you are about the sorriest thing I've seen In a long time, now get lost and leave me alone." she said.

"It's not because you're In a wheel chair Cathy." he said.

"Get lost." Cathy said.

As he walked away, tears started to well up In Cathy's eyes and she turned her head cause she didn't want him to know It. She finished her coffee and left. Soon she thought, If I can only find those people then maybe I can get a Doctor to listen to me. but I'm not doing it for people like that, I'm doing It for me. She got In her van and drove away, and as she was driving she passed Doctor Johnson's office and thought she would stop to see him so she parked the van and went In. The nurse came out and saw her and said.

"Cathy, I'll tell the Doctor you're here."

"Okay." she said.

"Cathy." Dr. Johnson said, "Come on In."

She wheeled In to one of the Inner offices and waited for him and when he came In he said.

"Now, I understand you are on a quest, how are you making out?"

"Fine, my dad and I talked to Doctor Franklin's grand daughter." she said.

"Did you?" he replied.

"Yes, and she gave us the names and addresses of seven people that dr. Franklin cured before he died." no kidding.

"Is that right?"

"Yes, that's right." she said.

"And who are these people?" he asked.

"Dad and I are starting a man hunt for these people, If I can find just one that's still alive." she said.

"Are they all In Deluth?" he asked.

"No, they're scattered all over." she said.

"Well, like I said, all It takes Is one person that I can talk to, and then It has to go through the proper medical channels and I don't know how long that would take." Dr. Johnson said.

"But you said," she asked.

"I know what I said and I will do what I said but It has to be done the right way." Dr. Johnson said.

"Well, I'm trying to find you one Oh great non believer." Cathy said.

"It's not that I don't believe Cathy, but the procedure has never been done that I know of and unless someone shows me how, I can't do It." the Dr. Said.

"I understand, wish me luck, I'm gonna need It." Cathy said.

"Good luck and I'll see you later, Bye Bye." He said.

When she got back to her van she was about to get In and her dad pulled up alongside and said.

"Cathy, leave the van and come with me, I want to buy you some lunch and I've got something to tell you."

He jumped out of his car and opened the trunk so he could put her chair In, he picked her up and placed her In the front seat and stored the chair In the trunk and they drove off. Del started by saying.

"Cathy, one of the people on the list lives right here In Deluth."

"You`re kidding?" she said.

"No, I asked a friend of mine to run the names on the list through his computer and one of the names on the list he says, lives right here In town, so, we'll have some lunch and we'll go check It out." Del said.

"Okay, right on dad, way to go, sounds good." Cathy said.

"Don't blow a gasket yet honey, he gave me an address and we can start there." Del said.

"What street Is It on?" she asked.

"Wilson lane." Del reported.

"I've never heard of It." she answered.

"Well lets have something to eat and we'll start looking." Del replied.

After lunch they started across town cause Del thought that he might have seen It over there somewhere, he said.

"It's got to be around here somewhere."

"Hey dad, there's a cop, lets ask him." she asked.

"Excuse me, but could you tell us where Wilson lane Is?" Del asked.

"Well, It use to be right there, pointing towards an overpass, but since they built the highway they did away with It years ago." he said.

"No Idea what happened to the people that lived on that street I suppose?" Del asked.

"Naw, It's been too long." the cop said.

"Okay, thank you." Del said.

"Well honey, where do we go now?" Del asked.

"I don't know daddy, I just don't know." Cathy said.

"I'm gonna try some of the neighbors, maybe someone might remember." Del said.

Del parked the car and walked up the steps of one house and rang the bell, a big man came to the door and Del said.

"Excuse me sir, my name Is Del Woods and I was wondering how long you have lived here on this street?

"All my life, why?" said the man.

"Well, I'm looking for a man that lived on Wilson Lane before they did away with It." Del added.

"What's his name?" he asked.

"George Fisher." Del said.

"Yeah I knew him but he passed away some years ago." he said.

"Gee, that's too bad, well thank you." Del said.

Del turned around and walked off the porch and back to the car to give Cathy the bad news. When he got to the car he said to Cathy.

"I'm afraid I have some bad news for you, the man I talked with said he knew him but he passed away some time back."

"Well, one down and six to go." Cathy said.

"You've got a lot of guts and I admire you for It." Del said.

"I told you daddy, I'm not giving up." Cathy said.

"At a go honey, but I think you had better check your list again, that's three down and four to go." Del said. "Oh yeah, you're right." Cathy said. "Well, tomorrow we start again." Del said. "Which one Is closest to us?" Cathy asked. "There's one In Jackson."

Said Del. "We'll go there tomorrow okay, now, which Is the next closest one?" asked Del. "There Is one In, oh, there's one just outside of Deluth." Cathy said. "Okay, we'll do those two tomorrow, okay?" Del asked. "Great." Cathy said. The next morning rolled around and Cathy wasn't feeling too good and Del said. "I'll go check those two out and you stay here and rest up, cause this has been quite a strain on you."

"Thanks daddy, you sure you don't mind?" Cathy asked. "Not at all honey, not at all." Del said.

Del jumped In his car and headed toward town, he thought, I'll try to see the one outside of Deluth first. so he drove to the address on the list and he found a big house that looked like one of those haunted houses you see In the movies, he walked up the long flight of stairs and finally reached a front porch, by that time he was pooped. He rang the bell and when the door started to open It sounded like Inner sanctum. An old grey haired lady came to the door and said. "Yes."

"Excuse me but, do you know a Wilma Jennings?" he asked.

"Yes." she said.

"Is there any way I could talk to her?" Del said.

"Not unless you go down to the old folks home, and even then, I don't think she would understand what you are saying." she said.

"How old Is she?" Del asked.

"Oh Lord, she must be 84 or 85 by now, I don't recall." she said.

"And which home Is she In?" Del asked.

"Birchwood Rest Home." she said.

After thanking the lady, Del got In his car and drove off toward town again cause that was where It was, he had seen It many times before. When he got there he started walking along a long walk that led to the front door and there laying near the walk was a big Great Dane just looking up at him, there was a man nearby who looked like a caretaker and he said.

"Don't worry bout him he ain't vicious."

"I sure hope not cause he's a big one." Del said.

He got to the door and rang the bell and a scrawny little woman came to the door with a smirk on her face and she looked like she hadn't had a good meal In months, and she said In a squeaky voice.

"Yeah, what can I do for you?" "I would like to see Wilma Jennings please." Del asked. "A lot of people would like to see Wilma Jennings, what do you want to see her for?" she asked.

"It's a long story." Del said. "Another one with a long story." she said.

"If I can't see her, can I see her Doctor?" Del asked.

"Come on In, I'll see what I can do for you." she said.

He followed her Into the Foyer and was told to wait there, A few minutes later an overweight man came over to him and said. "I'm Doctor Beasley, can I help you?" "I was hoping to get a chance to talk to Wilma Jennings." Del said. "What about?" the Doctor said.

"Well, she supposedly had an operation on her back some years ago and I was looking for evidence of that fact." Del said. "Are you a Doctor."

"Oh no sir, you see, my daughter had an accident and she can't walk and the Doctors tell her that they can't repair her back, and a Doctor James Franklin was suppose to have come up with a way to rejoin tendons and stuff." Del said.

"Now that you mention It, we had to take some x rays of her back last year and there was evidence of a back injury long before, but I didn't think anything of It at the time." the Doctor said.

"Do you think that you could get her to tell me about the operation?" Del asked.

"You're welcome to try, but I don't think you'll get far, she has Alzheimer's disease and she doesn't remember much." the Doctor said.

"Well I'd like to try anyway." Del asked

"If It's anything legal, I have a small cassette player and you can try to record what she tells you, cause sometimes she will give you an accurate answer the first time and can't repeat It." the Doctor said.

"Well, lets go see." Del said.

So Doctor Beasley Led him to a small room where Wilma was and there sat a lady that had seen too many years and was ready to go to her resting place. Del started to talk to her, he turned the recorder on and said.

"Hi Wilma, I'm Del Woods, Do you remember Dr. Franklin?" Del asked her.

"Yes, Dr. Franklin." "Now Wilma, do you remember the operation you had on your back." Del asked. "Yes, Dr. Franklin, how are you?" Wilma said. "I'm fine, do you remember when I gave you an operation on your back?" Del asked. "Yes, my operation, when Is It?" she said. "Do you see what I mean?" Dr. Beasley said. "Yeah, I see, Well we tried." Del said.

"Sorry you couldn't get the Information you were looking for." the Doctor said. "Oh that's all right Dr., you win some, you lose some." Del said.

Del was so hopeful, but he left there with his tail between his legs so to speak. He thought, four down and three to go, I don't know how we will ever find even one, everybody Is so old.

Chapter 7

Well, Buck up old boy, Cathy wouldn't quit, On to the next one. The address he had for the next one was on a country road outside of Deluth and there were no house numbers there, just Rural boxes. It was like trying to find a needle In a hay stack. He stopped at one house and didn't dare get out of the car because of a big dog that came running out when he pulled In, so he just blew the horn, An elderly man In his slippers came to the door and said. "Come on mister, go lay down rex, what can I do for you sonny?" When he saw a vast difference In age between Del and himself. "I'm looking for a Frank Jessie." Del asked. "Well, I don't think he's around anymore but he used to live two houses up from here on the same side of the road, What do you want him for?" he asked.

"Well, It's a long story and I'd like to tell you about It someday but right now I don't have the time, Thank you very much sir." Del said. And he walked away, wondering If he was gonna get the same story down the line. He stuck the key In the switch and the engine roared and he was gone. Down the road to the next place he went hoping that he would like to have some good news for his daughter Cathy when he got home. He pulled In to the driveway and got out and looked around to see if there were any dogs around but didn't see one so he went up the steps.

There was a small one sleeping on the porch that hadn't heard the car and when he woke up he jumped up and started to bark like crazy and gave Del quite a start. A woman came to the door and asked. "Can I help you?" "Maybe, I'm looking for a Frank Jessie." Del asked. "Dad, what do you want with him?" I'd like to talk with him If It would be possible?" he said.

"Well, yeah It's possible, come on In." she said. "Is he here?" Del asked.

"Yes he's In the living room." she said. Del thought, don't tell me I'm gonna get lucky. They rounded the corner Into the living room and there he was sitting In a wheel chair.

"Hi, I'm Del Woods, and I would Like to talk to you about Doctor James Franklin." Del said.

"Yeah, what about him?" He asked. "Is It true that you had an operation on your back performed by Dr. Franklin?" Del asked. "Yeah, It's true, a long long time ago." He said. "Could you tell me what happened." Del asked. "What's this all about any way and why the questions about Dr. Franklin?" he asked.

"My daughter was stabbed In the back and It left her a paraplegic, and we're trying to find some one that was operated on by Dr. Franklin because he was the only one that could perform the operation successfully." Del said.

"Yeah well, he operated on me and If I had listened to him and done what he told me I would be walking today." the man said.

"And what was It that you didn't do that he told you to do?" Del asked.

"After the operation he told me not to try to walk for one month, I was suppose to lie down on my back and not move and I got up too soon." you see, when I was a mere boy, I fell off of my dad's wagon, because I didn't sit down like he told me and I hit my back on a sharp rock and It went right In my back and cut everything, and Doctor Franklin knew It." He said.

"Did you go back to see him?" Del asked.

"Yes, but by the time I did he was dead." He said.

"You didn't go back right away?" Del asked

"No, I was too ashamed because I didn't listen to him." he said.

"Gee, that's too bad, so you're right back the way you were before the accident?" Del said.

"No, everything works except I can't walk." he said.

"So some of the repairs are still functioning?" Del asked.

"Oh yes." he said.

"Well sir, I thank you very much and I will be In touch with you If It's alright?" Del said.

"Any time." He said.

Del took down his name and address and phone number and left for home, It was about three In the afternoon and Del thought how good a hot cup of coffee would taste so he headed for the local hang out on Elm st. when he pulled In to the parking lot he thought he had seen Cathy's van and wondered If It was In fact hers, so he drove around the building and checked, yes, It was hers alright and he thought, good, I can fill her In on what has happened. When he walked In, Cathy's eyes lit up and she said.

"Hi, how did you make out?"

"Well, you might say I hit pay dirt." he said. Cathy screeched at the top of her lungs and Del said.

"Whoa girl, don't flip your lid, It`s very good but It could give us a problem." del said.

"What problem?" Cathy asked.

"Well, the first one I tried to talk to has Alzheimer's and couldn't tell me anything, and the second one told me that he did In fact have an operation by Dr. Franklin but he's In a wheel chair."

"How come?" she asked.

"Well, according to him, he didn't do what the Dr. told him and he ended up In the chair again, he didn't wait long enough after the operation and It messed It up but, he did walk." Del reported.

Cathy screamed again and said,.

"Dear Lord we're getting there."

"I'll have a coffee with you and we'll go see Doctor Johnson together." Del said.

Cathy started to cry and Del said.

"Take it easy honey, we've made some headway, but we're not there yet."

"I know, but I can feel It In my heart that we will make it." she said.

After their coffee Cathy got In with Del and they went to the Doctor's office. When they got there they went In and the nurse said.

"I'm sorry, Doctor Johnson Is gone for the day."

"Well, that's alright, we'll see him tomorrow then." Del said

Then Del said to Cathy,

"Lets go home, I'm bushed."

"Okay daddy, you've had a very fruitful day I would say." Cathy said.

They picked up the van and went home, and all that evening they talked about what had happened with the two people that Del had visited and the last one and what the possibilities were in that area. They all got a good night's sleep and the following morning Cathy and Del went to see Doctor Johnson. They were a little bit early so they went to the local coffee shop to kill some time and when they walked In, Cathy saw Bobby sitting there and when he saw Cathy he got up to leave and Cathy rolled over to where he was and said.

"You don't have to leave on my account Bobby." He never said a word, he just walked out. Del said.

"What was that all about?"

"Not too much dad, he doesn't want to be seen with me cause I'm In this chair." Cathy said.

"Well, I'm afraid there are a lot of people like that in this world baby." Del said.

Cathy said. "I know, I just didn't know that he was a fair weather friend."

"The truth you find out about your close friends can hurt sometimes." Del said.

"Tell me about It." Cathy replied.

Well, when they thought they had killed enough time they left and headed for the Dr.'s office. They got there and the Doctor was just coming In and he said.

"Cathy! Come on In."

Del pushed her In to the Inner office and waited, soon the Doctor came In and said.

"So, how are you doing with your man hunt?"

"We found one."

"You did?"

"Yes we did." Cathy said.

"And?"

"Well, the man Is In a wheel chair, but he told me that he's In there because he didn't listen to Doctor Franklin, He was suppose to stay on his back In bed for one month and he jumped the gun and got up, but, before his back let go again, he did walk."

"Your joking right."

"No sir I'm not." Del said. Plus, It left him better then he was before, he was able to get married and have a daughter, he has feelings in his legs and he has more function then before but he can't walk."

"How many do you have left on your list."

"Two, why?"

"I believe what you are telling me, but I would have a hard time to convince anyone with some one that's In a wheel chair." He continued, "Look, check out all your options and we'll take It from there, Okay?"

"Fine, we'll do that and we'll let you know how we make out." Cathy said.

"Lets go daddy."

They went back down to the coffee shoppe so they could sit down and talk about everything and Cathy started by saying.

"Lets go today daddy, we only have a couple of days left and you have to go back to work."

"Pass me your phone."

"Hi Deb. Cathy and I are going to Langly to see another one, I'll call you later, okay hun, bye."

"Now we're ready."

"Thanks daddy."

They drove to Langly and started looking for an Amy Webb, they went to the newspaper office and the hospital and the police dept. and couldn't find any trace of her what so ever, no one In town had ever heard of her.

Chapter 8

One police officer said that some years ago he had been called to settle a dispute out on an old country road and he thought that the woman's name was Amy. He gave them directions and they took off. They found the house In question but It was empty and had been for years, some said she had died and some said she had moved away, but they all said her name was Amy. So again, A dead end. Cathy said.

"Give It up daddy, lets go find the last one, if he Is still alive."

"Okay, we might as well."

"The last one lives or used to live In wellsley."

"Wells lezz go see."

"Cute daddy, I'll call mom and let her know what's going on."

"Fortunately for us these people all lived not too far away and we were able to follow up on all of them."

The drive to Wellsley took about two hours and when they got there Cathy said.

"Daddy, lets stop for something to eat, cause I don't think I can take another disappointment on an empty stomach."

"Okay, I'm hungry anyway."

They found a nice little restaurant In town and went In to eat. and Del said.

"If we don't get lucky with this one, all we have left Is the one In the wheel chair."

"You mean, that's all Doctor Johnson will have left, and I know what he wants, he wants some one to walk In to his office and say yes he did operate on me."

"I think you're right." Del said.

"Well, my fingers are crossed right to the end."

The waitress came over to their table and asked If she could help them, and Del said.

"Yes, we will order, but do you know a Robert White In town here?"

"Yes, Do you see that big grey house down the road there on the right side of the road?"

"Yes."

"Well, It's the next house after that one on the same side."

"Thank you very much."

They ordered their lunch and ate then started up the road to the house that the waitress had told them about. Del pulled Into the driveway and started looking around and Cathy said.

"What are you looking for daddy?"

"Does he have a dog?"

"I don't know but I'm not taking any chances." Del said.

"Why are you suddenly shy of dogs?" Cathy asked.

"Because I had a run In with a couple of them yesterday and It left me kinda jumpy." Del answered. They didn't see any dogs so he stopped the car and got out, and went up the steps to the front door, he knocked on the door and a man came out and said.

"Yes sir, what can I do for you?" the man said.

"We're looking for a Robert White, do you know him?" Del asked.

"Yes." the man said.

"Is there any chance we could talk to him?" Del asked.

"Well, that depends, who are you and what do you want him for?" he said. Del said. "I'm Del woods and that's my daughter Cathy there In the car, and she was Injured a while back and she can't walk, and we were told that this Robert White was operated on by a Doctor James Franklin and he could walk again, so could we talk to him?" Del said. "You are talking to him, I'm Robert White." he said. "Sir, could you come out to the car for a minute, there's some one who wants to meet you." Del asked. "Sure, no problem." he said.

So he walked down the steps and over to the car and Del said. "Cathy, this Is Robert White."

"Oh my god, don't tell me." Cathy cried.

"What's this all about." Robert asked.

"We've been looking for all the people that Doctor Franklin cured or repaired and you're the only one that we've found that Is still walking around." Cathy said.

"Could you tell us about the operation and why he had to perform It?" she asked.

"Well, why don't you come over to the picnic table here under this tree and we'll talk about It." Robert said.

So Del got the chair out of the trunk and they all migrated over to the table. He started by saying.

"You see, when I was very young I was riding on a wagon with my father and a snake scared the horses and they bolted and I fell off and the wagon wheel ran over my back and I couldn't walk, I was In a wheel chair just like you, until my father heard about Doctor Franklin and every one said that he was a quack, but my father said quack or no, I'm going to have him look at my boy." Robert went on. By this time Cathy's eye's were full of tears and so were Del's. He continued. "He told my father that the operation was not an accepted medical procedure, but he guaranteed results, so my dad told him to go ahead with the operation regardless of popular opinion."

"What were his Instructions after the operation." Del asked.

"He told my father that I had to lay on my back with a pillow under me for one month, then I could start to move a little at a time until I was able to get up and try to walk around." "And It worked?" Del asked. "Obviously, I'm sitting here without a wheel chair and talking to you, I was very stiff at first but my back got stronger and here we are." Cathy asked.

"Is there any way that we could get you to come to Deluth with us and meet my Doctor?" "Sure, but not today, I have an appointment this afternoon to get my glasses changed." he said.

"Well, tomorrow Is Friday and maybe we could come and pick you up and bring you over to Deluth with us." Del said.

"Yes but, we'd be late getting you back to Wellsley."

"That's no problem, cause I have a sister In Deluth and It would give me an excuse to visit with her and you can bring me back on Saturday." Robert said. "That would be wonderful, we'll be here tomorrow morning about 10:00." Del said.

Cathy had such a satisfied feeling on the way home that she slept all the way. Her dad woke her up In the driveway and she couldn't wait to get In the house and tell her mother about the good news. When she started to tell her, Debbie started to cry and she said.

"Dear God, do you think there' a chance." Del said.

"There' always a chance, but we'll see what Doctor Johnson has to say."

Cathy slept really good that night, In fact, better then she had since the accident, she woke up bright and early the next morning and knocked on her dad's door and said.

"I hate to wake you two up so early but we have a lot to do."

They all got up and had a good breakfast and Debbie said.

"Do you mind If I come with you today, I'd like to be In on this one." "I'd love It mom." Cathy answered. After breakfast they all got In the van and Del said. "You two sit In front, And I'm gonna lay down In the back seat, I didn't sleep too good last night, too much going on I guess." "That's okay daddy, We'll wake you when we get there." Cathy said. "Thanks." Del answered.

Actually, It gave Cathy and her mother a chance to talk that they hadn't had for quite a while. When they pulled In to town, Cathy called her dad and said.

"Dad, we're here, and I don't remember where that road Is." "Okay, I'll be right there." Del said.

Del went up front and looked out the windshield and said.

"Boy, If I ever want a good night's sleep, I'll know where to go, Okay turn left at this road here, and there's the house."

When Del knocked on the door, an old lady came out and said.

"Yes?"

"We came to pick up Mr. White." Del said.

"He called me this morning and said he wasn't feeling too good so I came over." the lady said. Just then, he came out to the door and said.

"Oh hi, I'll only be a minute." Robert said.

"But Robert, you said you weren't feeling good." the lady asked.

"I know, but this Is very Important to Cathy and after all, they are taking me to a Doctor, now don't you worry none, I'll be back tomorrow and I'll call you when I get back." Robert said.

They waited a few minutes and he came out with a small bag and said. "Let's go." Cathy said. "I'll be grateful to you for the rest of my life." "Cathy, stop where we stopped yesterday and we'll have some lunch." Del said.

"Okay daddy." Cathy replied.

Del said, "You will come In with us and have a bite won't you Mr. White?" "I might be talked Into It." he said.

"So they all went In and had lunch and It gave them an opportunity to talk about all sorts of things.

The drive to Deluth was very Interesting cause Robert was telling stories about the old days and for the first time In a very long time Del heard Cathy laugh, It was such a good sound and Del hadn't heard It In some time. Debbie thought how much laughing she would be doing If she can have the operation she's looking for. When they got to Deluth they went directly to Doctor Johnson's office. Robert said. "You know something, I feel better." "That's great." Cathy said. They went In and sat down and Del let the nurse know that they were there and she said. "I'm sorry but It will be A while cause he's very busy today." Del said. "That's perfectly alright, we'll wait."

After about an hour of waiting, Del went down stairs to the pop machine and got everybody a pop and told them that he would take the bottles back down when they got done. Del said to Cathy, "It might be quite a while cause he takes people by appointment only as a rule."

"Yes I know, but some times when he's not too busy he takes me right away." Cathy said. Just then he came out of one of the inner offices and spotted Cathy, and said.

"Cathy! wait one more minute." Dr. Johnson said.

Chapter 9

He turned and told his nurse to put Cathy In the next room available, and there was one empty so she called Cathy In. Cathy said.

"I'm sorry but, we all have to go In." Cathy asked.

"Okay Cathy, there's enough room I think." she said.

"Daddy, when Dr. Johnson comes In, let me do the talking please." Cathy asked.

"It's your ball game sweetie." Del said.

Just then the door opened and Dr. Johnson said.

"Hail Hail the gang's all here, how's It going Cathy."

"Doctor Johnson, this Is Mr. Robert White."

"Hi, how are you." he said.

"I'm very well, thank you." he said.

"Dr. Johnson, this the list of people that Dr. Franklin cured, would you read It please?" Cathy asked.

"Sure, Hey, are you the Robert White on this list?" he asked.

"One and the same." Robert said. "Were you?" he asked. "A paraplegic, yes I was, until Dr. Franklin operated on me." Robert answered.

"I have a small x ray machine In the back room, would you allow me to take an x ray of your back." the Doctor asked.

"Right now? Sure." Robert said.

After that Dr. Johnson came out and said.

"This granddaughter of Dr. Franklin's, would she have procedural records?" Cathy said.

"I believe she does." "Could you get me a copy?" Doctor Johnson asked. "If she has them, sure." Cathy said. "How soon could you get me a copy." Doctor Johnson asked.

"By Monday soon enough." Cathy asked.

"Well, If that Is the soonest." the Doctor said.

"What's got you so gung ho." Cathy said.

"I'm sorry, at first I didn't believe you, and then as you kept digging Into It, I began to think that you were probably on to something, and now you brought me some one that was operated on by this Dr. Franklin and I'm glad that I'm In on this thing, not only could It bring recognition to Dr. Franklin but I could become famous, If I can sell the American Medical Association. The Doctor said.

"So now you believe me." Cathy said.

"Yes, and after I have read the procedural records I will give you my findings and weather I think Dr. Franklin was a quack or not." Doctor Johnson said.

"That's fine with me." said Cathy.

When Robert came back from the back room, Dr. Johnson asked him If he was gonna be In town on Saturday and he said.

"I'll be here till 3:00 tomorrow afternoon."

"Would you meet with me tomorrow morning so we could talk about everything?" the Doctor asked. "Sure Doc. when and where?" Robert asked. "Where will you be staying?" the Doctor asked. "In the old Fabrics building apt 4." Robert said. "Okay, I'll pick you up about 9:00 AM and we'll go to breakfast, Okay?" Doctor Johnson said.

"Sure, fine, this must be big, everybody buying me breakfast." Robert said. Cathy picked up her phone and called Alice Bains and ask her If she could have a copy of the procedural records and she said. "No problem Cathy, when do you want to pick them up?"

"I'd like to come up tomorrow If It's okay." Cathy said.

"Sure, that will be fine, listen, why don't you make It around noon and we'll do lunch." Alice said. "Oh, I'd like that." Cathy replied. The Alice said. "Fine, I'll see you then." Cathy turned to Del and said.

"Alice wants me to have lunch with her tomorrow."

"Hey, That's great honey, I suppose you two do have a lot to talk about, will you be okay to drive out there by yourself?" Del asked.

"Oh sure, It's time I stretched my legs with that new van anyway." Cathy said.

"Yeah, I guess so but you be careful." Del said.

"I will daddy." Cathy replied.

Dr. Johnson said.

"Well Cathy, It's up to me now, the ball Is In my court and I will do my best to convince the A. M. A, I just hope they don't think I'm a quack."

"I certainly hope that they don't." Cathy answered.

Well, they all thanked Robert very much and Cathy asked him If she could drop him off home on her way to see Alice and he said. "It's out of your way Isn't It?" "Nothing Is out of my way, after what you did for me." Cathy said., "what time are you leaving?" Robert asked. "about 10:00 tomorrow morning."

"Fine then, I'll be ready to leave as soon as Dr. Johnson is done with me." he said. "Great". Cathy said. It was a little bit out of her way but Cathy didn't mind one bit to take him home again, after all, he came all the way out here to help her and that Is something she could never repay.

Robert turned to Dr. Johnson and said. "You had better pick me up at eight If you feel like talking cause I'm leaving at ten."

"That'll be fine." said Dr. Johnson. "It's my day off but I'll be there cause I very much feel like talking."

Well, the leg work on Cathy's part was done, and done well If I must say, now It was Up to the Lord and Dr. Johnson.

Del dropped Robert off at his sister's place and gave him his name and address and phone number in case something went wrong and he needed help, Robert thanked him and assured him that everything was going to be alright. Then, Cathy, Del and Debbie went home and It never looked so good, cause they were all very tired, Brenda met them at the door and wanted to know everything and Cathy said come In to my room and I'll fill you In on all the latest dirt. That's the way the kids there talked, meaning "Information."

They talked for about two hours and Cathy said.

"I'm awful tired Brenda, can we continue this conversation tomorrow?"

"Oh sure Cathy, I'm sorry, but I'm so happy for you." Brenda said.

"Oh Brenda, would you like to come with me tomorrow, I have to go see Alice and take Robert home." Cathy asked.

"I'd love to Cathy, I thought you'd never ask." Brenda replied.

"Then It's settled, I'll wake you up at eight." Cathy said. "Ouch." Brenda said.

The next morning Cathy got up as usual, and as she had done the better part of her life, without an alarm clock and knocked on Brenda's door and a strange moan came from Inside and Cathy knew that she would have to knock again, so bang bang bang, and Del said. "Hey you girls, what's going on down there?" "I'm trying to wake Brenda up daddy." Cathy said.

"I'll get her up for you." Del said. Del got up and got dressed and came downstairs and tapped on Brenda's door and said.

"Brenda, come on, It's time to get up." Brenda answered, "Okay daddy, I'll be right there."

"You see Cathy, It's got to be the right voice." Del said.

"Yeah, I guess so, you want a cup of coffee ?" Cathy asked.

"I might as well now that I'm up." Del said.

"Listen, you girls will be careful today." Del asked.

"Yes we will, I don't Intend to drive fast." Cathy said.

"I know you're not a fast driver but sometimes It's not you, you have to have eyes In the back of your head." Del said.

"I know, one cut In front of me on main street the other day and I had to slam on the breaks to keep from hitting him." Cathy said.

"It's a good thing you learned the controls like you did Eh?" Del asked. Brenda came In, eyes half shut and said.

"What time Is It anyway?" Cathy asked her dad.

"It's 8:20 and you had better get ready If you're going." Del said.

Cathy said. "Yeah, okay." "Cathy, do you want me to make you two some breakfast?" Del asked. "No daddy, we're having breakfast with Dr. Johnson and Mr. White. "I'm still pursuing daddy, I can't change." Cathy answered.

"Lord I wouldn't want you to, I love you just the way you are."

"I love you too." Cathy said.

Brenda came in all dressed and said.

"I'm ready Ramrod."

"In that case, MUSH." Cathy replied.

"You two are something else." Del said.

They piled In to the van and drove off and Debbie said.

"Del?"

"Yes." he answered.

"Are the girls gone?" Debbie asked.

"They're just pulling out now." Del said.

"Come on back to bed." Debbie asked Del.

"Best offer I've had all day, here I come." he said.

When they walked in to the restaurant they were both there and Dr. Johnson said.

"Good Morning girls, sit down and have some breakfast, it's on me."

Cathy laughed and said.

"Lets take him up on it, that may be all I`ll ever get out of him."

Brenda laughed and they sat down. "Good morning Cathy." Mr. White said. "Good morning sir, been here long?" Cathy asked. "Since about 8:00." Dr. Johnson said. "This man has told me stories about Dr. Franklin that has changed my opinion of him completely." Dr. Johnson said.

"No kidding?" Cathy asked.

"I'm not kidding at all, that man was demeaned unjustly, people condemned him because his methods were different, but apparently effective." Dr. Johnson said.

"My goodness, all that from one breakfast chat?" Cathy asked.

"It's unfortunate now that someone else will take the credit for his work." Dr. Johnson said.

"Oh no, there is no one taking credit for Doctor Franklin's work, I'm dealing with his granddaughter, and she will not allow that to happen, and I wouldn't want her to, that man suffered enough at the hands of the public for his work to be ignored now." Cathy said.

"I didn't mean It like that Cathy, but If his work is to be accepted by the A.M.A, It will have to be Introduced to them by someone here today." Johnson said. "I'm sorry Dr. I guess I'm getting jumpy." "That's okay Cathy, listen, when are you coming back?" the Dr. Asked. "This afternoon, why?" Cathy asked. "Would you mind another passenger?" the Dr. Asked. "Who?" asked Cathy "Me." the dr. said. "Why?, do you want to meet Alice?" Cathy asked.

"Yes I do, If I'm to present this to other Doctors of my peers, I need all the Information I can get, could I use your phone for a moment?" he asked. "Sure." Cathy said.

Chapter 10

He dialed the number to his house and advised his wife that he was going with us and not to worry.

"Now, Cathy, I'm paying for this trip so when you stop for gas or lunch or what ever, I'm paying," the Dr. Said.

"If you say so but the van Is full already and so am I now." Cathy said.

"Well, we'll fill you up when we return, how's that?" the Dr. Said.

"That's fine by me." Cathy replied.

"This way I'll have more time to talk to Mr. White also." the Dr. Said.

So, Cathy, Brenda, Mr. White and Dr. Johnson all got In the van and went off down the road. They drove for about two hours and Cathy recognized the area and said.

"We're starting up the mountain to castle hill and I'm going to stop for a coffee before I go see Alice, Is that okay with everybody?" They all said It was alright, Robert White had gone to Castle Hill with them because he wanted to meet Alice and asked Cathy If she could drop him off on the way back. Dr. Johnson was surprised to know that they were almost there cause he had talked all the way and time just flew. Cathy and

Brenda caught up on a lot of things that they hadn't had time to talk about for a long time, and Brenda said.

"You drive this rig very good I find, It didn't take you long to learn."

"Well, I studied the thing for about a week before I took It out on the road." Cathy said. "Still, It must be hard to drive just with your hands." Brenda replied.

"A bit, but I heard that they are working on one now that you put a band around your head and what you are thinking, that's what the van will do." Cathy said. "No kidding?" Brenda replied.

"Yes, but I don't Intend to drive with my hands all my life." Cathy said. "Well, for your sake, I hope you make It."

"Here we are folks, Bens luncheonette, everybody out." Cathy said.

"I'm so very glad I came with you on this trip, cause It gave me a chance to see just how much moxie you really have, a lot more then I gave you credit for Cathy." Doctor Johnson said.

After the coffee break, Cathy drove over to Alice's house and a woman that was there said she had gone to the market for some groceries and she shouldn't be long. Cathy said.

"That's okay, we'll wait."

The house where Alice lived didn't have a front porch, just a one step 4 x 4 cement slab, and she thought that maybe the good ole Doctor could haul her Inside. A few minutes went by and Cathy saw a small grey car pull up In the drive and from where she was she saw that It was Alice, She got out of the car and yelled.

"Hi Cathy."

"Hi Alice, I brought you some company." Cathy said.

"Oh, That's great, let me bring In my bags and I'll make some tea." Alice said.

After she got all her stuff In the house she turned to the gang and said.

"Would you gentlemen like a beer or something?"

Both Dr. Johnson and Mr. White said that It would be great. Cathy started by saying,

"Alice, this Is Dr. Johnson, he will be operating on me If we can pull this off. "Hi, how are you?" Alice said. "I'm fine, thank you." the Dr. Said. "And this Is Mr. Robert White." the Dr. Pointed out. "The Robert White from the list?" she asked. "One and the same." Robert said.

"My God, I didn't think that any of my grandfather's patients were still alive, It certainly Is a pleasure to meet you." Alice said. "The pleasure Is all mine." Robert said. Mr. White said as they shook hands.

"Now, To what do I owe this unexpected pleasure?" Alice asked. "I came to get your grandfather's notes on the operation and Doctor Johnson wanted to meet you and so did Mr. White." Cathy said.

"Well, lets start with the records, I'll get them." Alice said.

She came back and handed them to Dr. Johnson and said.

"I suppose you are the only one here that would understand these so here they are."

He took them and went over to a chair that was by a window and sat down and started to read. Cathy and Alice were yakin a mile a minute about all sorts of stuff and Mr. White was watching T.V.. After about a half hour, Dr. Johnson got up and said.

"Cathy, I'm not too well versed on this procedure, but It could work."

"It does work." said Mr. White.

"Yeah, I guess It does, you're living proof of that aren't you?" Dr, Johnson said.

"You bet." said Robert.

"Alice, can you make me a copy of all these?" the Dr. Asked.

"Sure, If you don't mind waiting a few minutes, I have to go to the library, there's a copier there and It's just across the street." Alice said. "That's no trouble at all, we'll wait." the Dr. Said. She grabbed all the notes and said. "I'll be back In a minute."

"Cathy, I haven't read all the procedural records yet, I figured I'd do that on the way back, but If It's what I think It Is, It will work."

"That's the best news I've heard In years." Cathy said.

"Of course remember now, we still have to convince the A.M.A." Dr. Johnson said.

"Yes I know." Cathy replied.

"If they say no and I do It anyway, then I'm a quack." the Dr. Said.

Cathy said. "I'm aware of that too." "Although, If they are against It and I do It anyway, they can bring charges against me for going against them, but If I prove them wrong, I would win In court anyway." the Dr. Said.

"It's quite a big step for you Isn't It?" Cathy asked. "Good size, but then, I'm a gambler, always have been. You see, every person's metabolism Is different, and some times one of my patient's will say, that a certain medicine works for them and It's not the recommended medicine for what ails them, I tell them, If It works for you, Take It." the Dr. Said. "Not all Doctor's would do that." Cathy said. "No, I check them over and If I think the medicine Is working, I allow It, A man came to me with a sort of fungus under his foot and I honestly didn't know what it was, so I took a culture and sent It to a lab, and a couple of days later, the man called me and said he had healed It with Unguentine, which Is found In sunburn lotion, go figure." the Dr. Said. "But you're not prescribing bad medicine, you're going with the flow, If It works don't knock It."

Cathy said.

"Exactly, Another example, A woman came to me with this redness all over her face and I sent her to a specialist, A little while later, she called to tell me that she cured It with hemorrhoidal medicine." Dr. Johnson said.

"I think I know what you are saying, what's not good for the Goose, may be good for the Gander." Cathy said.

"Right on Cathy." the Dr. Said.

Just about then, Alice came In with the records In a brown envelope and said.

"Here you are Dr., I hope this works for you."

"I think It will." he said.

"Cathy, let me know when you get operated on, I'd like to be there." Alice said.

"I can't think of anyone that I would want there more." Cathy said.

"Not even me?" Brenda said. "Oh, you know what I mean." Cathy replied.

"Yes I do, just kidding." Brenda replied.

"Let me know too will you Cathy, I'd like to be there also." Mr. White said.

"I certainly will Mr. White, you've been a darling all through this." Cathy replied.

"First time I've been called a darling In years, the trip was well worth my time, thank you." Robert said.

"You're welcome." Cathy replied.

"Well, We got what we came for so we had better go cause I have to take Mr. White home yet." Cathy said.

"Where does he live?" Alice asked.

"Wellsley." Cathy replied.

"Well, Isn't this a coincidence, I have to go there this afternoon so I can take him home, But, before you go Cathy, we were suppose to do lunch." Alice said.

"Oh yes, I almost forgot." Cathy said..

"It's on me." said Dr. Johnson

Mr. White said.

"I don't care who It's on, lets go eat."

They all laughed and Alice knew of a nice restaurant In Castle Hill and she took them there. Mr. White said.

"Ain't never been In a place this fancy before."

"You sound like an old, hayseed." Cathy said.

He laughed and Grabbed Cathy's wheel chair and started to pull It over the step that went Inside and suddenly he grabbed his chest and Cathy said.

"Doctor." Dr. Johnson put his arms around him and sat him down on a bench by the door, and said. "Hey, what's the problem here." "Oh, It's just my old ticker, I'm not suppose to exert myself at all, according to my Dr.." Robert said.

"I think he's right Robert." the Dr. Said.

Chapter 11

A man came out the door and asked If he should call a Doctor and Dr. Johnson said.

"I am a Doctor." "Oh, okay." "How do you feel now Robert?" the Dr. Asked. "Good enough to go eat." Robert said.

"If I was you I'd listen to my Doctor." Doctor Johnson said. "What's your first name anyway, all through this trip It's been Dr. Johnson this and Dr. Johnson that and you call everybody by their first names." Robert asked.

"Oh I'm sorry, I never gave It a thought, My name Is Al, Al Johnson." the Dr. Said.

"There now, that didn't hurt a bit did It?" Robert said.

"You're something else, I'm very glad I met you all, you've made my life richer." the Dr. Said.

"I hope you're richer cause you're paying for the lunch." Cathy said. again they all laughed.

Al on one side of Bob, and Brenda on the other and they went In to the restaurant and sat down. Al said.

"Robert, do you take nitro pills?" the Dr. Asked.

"No, he never gave me any." Robert chided. "What's his name?" the Dr. Asked.

"Dr. Frank Waddel." "I'd like to talk to him If you don't mind." Dr. Johnson asked. "Not at all." said Robert.

"Hey you guys, I'm hungry." said Brenda, "Me too." said Cathy.

"Well, that's a good sign." Al said. "Oh by the way Alice, did you know your grandfather?" Al asked.

"Not that I recall, I think I must have been too young to remember, My mom told me a lot about him though, she said people used to laugh at him cause his methods were different, but he was the only Dr. In town that got results and she figured that the rest were jealous." Alice said.

"That may not be as far fetched as you might think." Al said.

"back then they didn't have any Medical Association to answer to, and If any Doctor came up with a better way, he was called a quack." Al said.

Well, after they all had their fill of good food, they said their goodbyes and Cathy pointed the van towards Deluth and they took off. On the way home Dr. Johnson read all the way back, and at one point Cathy asked.

"What do you think Doc?" "I think the man was a genius." Al said.

"That good eh?" said Cathy. "Better then that." Al replied.

"You still think It's possible?" asked Cathy.

"Oh yeah, according to this It's a very simple procedure, I'm surprised that someone hasn't thought of It." Al said.

"Well, maybe Doctors are afraid to take on the A.M.A." Cathy added.

"I sure hope you don't have too much trouble with them." Brenda said.

"I don't think I'll have to do too much convincing with this text, I know someone there, and that Is where I'm going to start, first thing Monday morning." Al said.

"Well, I'm glad that I'm the one that turned you on, so to speak." Cathy said, laughing.

Cathy drove Dr. Johnson back to the restaurant where he had left his car that morning when they got In to Deluth and wished him luck.

"Thank you very much for a very beautiful day, I've learned more today then I have In a long time, thank you." Al said.

"You're welcome, keep me posted please." Cathy replied.

"I will be In close contact with you, and stop In any time." Al said. "Bye." Cathy said. "See ya." Al replied.

Cathy was anxious to get home so she could tell her mom and dad about her day. "I'm gonna tell mom and dad about everything that happened today." Brenda said.

"No you don't you traitor, I want to do that." Cathy added.

"I wouldn't steel your thunder sis, just kidding." Brenda said.

They pulled Into the yard and Del and Debbie came running out all worried and they said. "What happened to your phone?" Del asked.

"Why?" Cathy asked.

"Cause we tried to call you and we couldn't get through." Del said.

Cathy picked up her phone and said.

"Oh, I'm sorry, It's turned off."

"I want to tell you, you girls gave us quite a scare." Dell said.

"Sorry daddy, It's all Brenda's fault." Cathy said.

"Yeah right Cathy." Brenda added

Cathy laughed and said.

"Daddy, could you push me In to the house, I'm pooped."

"I believe It honey, I guess you've had a full day." Del said.

"Better then that daddy, better then that." Cathy replied.

"Now you've got my undivided attention." Del added.

"We'll talk during supper, right now I have to go to the little girls room." Cathy said. "Okay baby," Del replied.

"Mom, I have to lay down for a while." Cathy said.

"Okay honey, I'll wake you for supper." her Mom said.

"Cathy has a lot to tell you about what happened today and I promised her I would let her tell you or she'll kill me." Brenda said. "That's okay babe, we'll wait for her to tell us If that Is the way she wants It." her Mom said. "Mom, I've never seen anybody with such a drive, you'd think that a person In her condition would be a bit Invalid us, but no way, she's Inexhaustible." Brenda said.

"She's a woods Isn't she, look at your father, there's not a lazy bone In that mans body, he's a good father and a good provider." Debbie said.

"We're very fortunate to have the parents that we have, cause I've seen a lot of bad ones." Brenda said.

"Thank you honey, I'm glad you feel that way." said Debbie.

Supper time rolled around and Debbie went In and woke Cathy up and said.

"Sorry honey, I know you're very tired but maybe some supper will do you good." Debbie said. "Okay mom, I'll be right there." Cathy replied.

"You want some help?" Debbie asked. "No thanks." Cathy added.

Cathy went In to the bathroom and then to the kitchen and up to the table, and when everybody was seated she started to tell them about what had happened during the day and they were both ecstatic. Del said.

"When will Dr. Johnson let you know?"

"Lord only knows, he has to battle the A.M.A and he's got his work cut out for him, but he told me that even If they refuse the proposal, he feels that he could perform the operation anyway." Cathy said. "You're kidding?" Del said, "what turned him on?" "The records we got from Alice, he read them and said that the procedure Is fairly simple." Cathy replied.

"Is that what Dr. Franklin called Fusion?" Del asked.

"Yes, Dr. Johnson said according to the records that you just tie the main cables together and the rest take care of themselves, those are not the right terms and It's not that easy but basically That's what It Is." Cathy replied.

"Well, for what we know about medical procedures, which Is not much, I'll buy that." Del said.

"Dr. Johnson explained It to me In layman's terms." Cathy said.

Well, after supper Cathy said, "I don't want to go anywhere tonight, I just want to sit here and watch T.V. to get my mind off of medical stuff."

"No problem Cathy, we weren't planning to go out tonight anyway." Del said.

"Well If nobody minds I've got a date and I will be going out." Brenda said.

"Not too late babe, you've had a long day too." Debbie said. "Okay, I'll be home early, about five In the morning." Brenda laughed.

"Yeah right." Debbie said. "Just kidding," I won't be late." Brenda replied.

About a week went by and Cathy decided to touch base with Dr. Johnson, so she got In her van and drove down to his office A man opened the door so she could go In and the receptionist said. Cathy,

I'll tell the Dr. you're here."

A few minutes went by and he came out of one of the small examination rooms and said.

"Cathy,! come on In."

She went In to the small room and he came In and sat down and Cathy said.

"How did you make out,?" she asked.

"Don't ask, they already think I'm nuts, I had to go and fill out some forms and now I have to wait for them to review the whole thing before I hear anything, they had to have copy's of the copy's and they may need an affidavit from Alice to verify the authenticity of the documents." said Al.

"They're giving you a run for your money aren't they?" Cathy added

"And If I do the operation with out their consent they can fine me, $500,000.oo just like that." Al said. and he snapped his fingers.

"So what are you going to do?" Cathy asked. "Just wait and see what they say." Al said.

"And how long will that take?" Cathy asked. "Lord only knows, could take months." Al said. "Oh God, after all that hard work and to have come so far, just to be Immured by the A.M.A." Cathy said.

"I know what you mean, but there's not much we can do." Al said.

"I thought my work was finished, but I guess not." Cathy said.

"What are you going to do Cathy?" Al asked.

"I'll wait for a while, and if they drag their feet, I have another ace up my sleeve." Cathy said. "I figured you would have." Al added.

"I told you before Doc. I'm not giving up." Cathy told him.

"The first ace you had did a fantastic job, let's see what this one does." Al said. Another two weeks went by and Cathy was still waiting patiently to hear something from the Doctor and she hadn't heard anything, so she called him one afternoon and said. "Hi, Doctor Johnson, It's Cathy, have you heard anything?" "You must have a sixth sense, I just got off the phone with them and they want to see me tomorrow." Al said. "Really?" Cried Cathy

"Yes, and I'm sure they've had time to read the records by now, so I can only assume that they want to talk to me about them." Al said.

"Good Lord, go, and let me know what happens." Cathy almost crying.

"You'll be the first to know Cathy." Al said. "Thanks, bye."

Cathy told her mom she was going to the coffee shop to be with the girls and clear her head, Debbie said.

"Go ahead hon, God knows you need a diversion after what you've been through."

"I won't be too long mom." Cathy said.

"Okay hon, take your time."

Chapter 12

Cathy drove that van out of the driveway like a pro. and headed down town. She got to the shop and all the girls were there and just having a ball, they all yelled "Cathy", when she rolled In. She went over to the table where the girls were and one of them asked her If she wanted a cup of coffee, and she said.

"Oh yes, I need It to calm my nerves."

The girl Barbra said. "I'll go get you one."

"That's okay, I'll get It." Cathy said.

Another girl, Janice, motioned to Barbra with a gesture with her head, that said don't do It. Cathy got herself a cup and a donut and went back to sit down with the girls. One of them said.

"Hey Cathy, I hear you went to Castle Hill with Doctor Johnson?"

"Are you on a digging expedition?" she asked.

"No," Cathy replied. "I was just asking, I didn't mean any thing by It." the girl said.

"Okay, fine, we went to Castle Hill to get some medical records, Me, him, Brenda and a Mr. Robert White." Cathy said.

"I didn't mean to Imply." the girl said.

"That's perfectly alright, some day I'll explain the whole thing to you so you don't go off half cocked." Cathy said.

"Gees, I'm sorry." the girl said.

"It's okay, but If you're gonna shoot a gun, make sure It's fully loaded." Brenda said.

Well, after that they all settled down to telling stories and jokes and laughing like crazy. Cathy didn't carry a grudge, she said what was on her mind and that was that. They had a ball, and Cathy really needed that, she laughed so hard that her wheel chair started to move and that made the other girls laugh all the more. By the time Cathy left the coffee shop she was completely unwound. She drove home and was telling her mom about her meeting with the girls, and her dad walked In and said.

"Have you heard?" Del asked. "Heard what?" Cathy asked.

"Doctor Johnson was in a car accident tonight." Del said. "How is he?" Cathy asked. "Don't know, they took him to the hospital." Del said.

"Dad, let's go." Cathy said.

"Okay my little chickadee, lets." Del replied.

"We'll take the van." Cathy said.

"I'm going too." said Brenda.

They got to the hospital and the nurse on duty said.

"I'm sorry, but you can't go in to see him cause they're only letting family in to see him."

"How is he?" Cathy asked.

"A bit shaken up, but other then that he's fine." the nurse said.

"Will he have to stay in the hospital for long?" Cathy asked.

"No, he'll be released tonight, for now he's resting. The nurse said. "Would you do me a favor, tell him that Cathy was here." "I'll go tell him right now." the nurse said. "Thanks." replied Cathy.

She turned her chair around and started to head for the elevator and the nurse yelled.

"Cathy, oh Cathy."

Cathy turned around again and the nurse motioned her to come back, the nurse said.

"He wants to see you." "Okay, thank you." Cathy said.

Del pushed her in to the room and there he was laying on the bed with all his clothes on, and he said.

"Cathy, come on over here."

"How are you?" Cathy said.

"Oh, I'm fine, they just wanted to keep me here for a while to see if there would be any complications." Al said.

"What happened?" Cathy asked.

"I stopped at a light and I got rear ended." Al said.

"You didn't get whip lash did you?" Cathy asked.

"I don't know, it's too early to tell." Al replied.

"You still going to the A.M.A tomorrow?" Cathy asked.

"Wild horses couldn't keep me away." Al said.

"Listen, if you need my help, let me know okay?" Cathy asked.

"I certainly will." Al said.

Cathy, Del and Brenda said their goodbye's and left.

The next day Cathy was on pins and needles waiting to hear from Dr. Johnson. About 4:30 the phone rang and it was Dr. Johnson, and he said.

"They want to set up a meeting with everyone concerned, Mr. White, Alice, you, and me. they want to discuss the possibilities of a new breakthrough in medical science." Dr. Johnson said.

Cathy let out the loudest scream, and the whole family came running toward her and wanted to know what happened.

She was shaking like a leaf and she said.

Dr., I'll call you or better yet, I'll come in to see you tomorrow."

"Okay Cathy, I'll see you then." he replied.

Still shaking, she tried to tell her mom and dad what Dr. Johnson had said and she was having a hard time, she started to hyperventilate and Del got scared and ran in the kitchen and got a paper bag cause he saw it on T.V. once and made her breath in it. She started to calm down and was able to get out a few words about her news. Del said.

"My God, I would have done the same thing with news like that, that's fantastic, when?"

"I don't know, Oh daddy, it's all coming together." Cathy said.

"And you made it happen honey, it's a result of your hard work." Del added.

"And yours, I want to take this opportunity to thank all of you for helping me with this." Cathy said.

"There is still a possibility that they wont accept it isn't there?" Debbie asked.

"I don't know, Dr. Johnson sounded pretty positive." said Cathy.

"We're not trying to discourage you by any means but we want to explore all avenues." Del asked.

"I know daddy, and you couldn't discourage me even if you did try." Cathy said. "Now that's the truth." Del replied.

"Listen, what do you say we all go down to Gino's and have a pizza, on me." Del said.

"I'm in, but you're gonna look awful silly with pizza all over you daddy." Cathy replied.

"Cute Cathy, cute, come on you guys, let's go." Del said.

They all went down for some pizza and Cathy was one big smile, a couple of her girlfriends were there with their dates and one of them came over and said. "You look happy tonight."

"I am, I can't really talk about it but I got some good news today." Cathy said.

"Hey, great." the girl answered.

"What are you guys up to?" Cathy asked.

"Oh nothing, we just went to the movies." she said.

"Anything good." Cathy asked.

"No, a flick called, "THE MONSTER IN YOUR BED." she said.

"no good huh?" Cathy asked.

"Well, if you like that kind of thing, today that's all boys want to see, sex. sex, sex." she said.

"I know, I don't like that either." Cathy said.

"Well, I'll see you later Cathy." the girl said. "Yeah, bye." Cathy replied.

Cathy turned to her mom and dad and said. "She's very nice." "Most of your friends are from what I've seen Cathy." Del said.

"I don't like gossips and I don't like people with bad mouths, and I don't hang around with them, boys turned me off in school when I was going, all they could talk about was sex, I might enjoy it some day too but I don't want to talk about it all day every day." Cathy said.

"Well." Del said. "I'm learning something about my daughter, I knew there was a reason why I loved you so much."

"If it wasn't for the love you have for me, and I for you, I probably wouldn't be the way I am." Cathy said.

"Well, that convince's me that I have a pretty wonderful daughter." Debbie said.

"Hey, what am I, Swiss cheese?" Brenda retorted.

"I meant both of you." Debbie said. "Okay, that's better." Brenda said.

"You missed your vocation Brenda." Del said. "You should have been a comic." "Ha, Ha,"

It was a good time for Cathy to unwind cause everybody was in a good mood and they were having fun just being with each other. Cathy had brought her phone with her, unbeknown to her cause she had forgotten that it was in her jacket pocket and it started to ring, and everybody was stunned, Cathy answered it and it was Dr. Johnson, he asked Cathy if she could call Mr. White and Alice and put them on stand by just in case. Cathy said.

"Yeah, no problem, do you think it will be soon?" Cathy asked.

"I don't know but I want to be ready." Al said.

"Okay, consider it done." Cathy said. "Thank you Cathy." Al said.

The drive back home Cathy was very relaxed still very happy for what had happened and more hopeful then she had been in a very long time. Her dad said.

"If everybody had your courage, things would get done in this world, people accept way more then they should."

"Well, I don't know about everyone else daddy, I just know about how I feel." Cathy answered.

"You've always been a go getter, you never let anything stand in your way, you drive right in there head long." Del said.

"Maybe it's because I'm a Taurus, the bull." said Cathy.

"Yeah, maybe so honey." Del said with a chuckle.

When they got home and settled in, Cathy talked on the phone for about an hour and never once talked about her situation in the course of the conversation, she wasn't one to look for sympathy from anyone, It was what it was, and that was that.

The next morning after breakfast she called Alice at the library and asked her if it would be possible for her to come to Deluth if the A.M.A needed her to do so, she said.

"No problem, for you and for gramps, any time, you just let me know."

"Thank you very much Alice, you don't have to worry about a motel if you should stay overnight because I would want you to stay with us here at home, we have an extra bedroom and it's very comfortable." Cathy said.

"Oh, thank you very much, I'd like that." Alice said.

"We'd spend the whole night talking." Cathy said.

"Listen, I have to go now, my boss just walked in, let me know okay?" Alice said.

"Okay I will, bye." Cathy replied.

She hung up and called Mr. White and he said.

"Fine but you'll have to pick me up and bring me back home again."

Cathy said. "That's no problem at all Mr. White, I'll do that gladly."

Another two weeks went by and Cathy was getting bored just hanging around the house doing nothing, and that just wasn't Cathy, she had to keep doing things all the time.

That Thursday afternoon Dr. Johnson called and said.

"Cathy, can you get your people ready for Monday morning?"

"Yes I can." Cathy replied.

"Have them all here in Deluth for Monday morning and I will meet you at that same restaurant that we met at before at 9:00 A.M. sharp, cause we have to be at the A.M.A at 10:00 okay?" Al said.

Chapter 13

"Okay, I'll be there, and thank you," Cathy replied. Cathy called Alice back again and Mr. White also and it was all set. Alice said that she would leave on Sunday and that she would call when she got in town, and Mr. White said he would be ready to go any time Sunday.

"Okay, I'll be there Sunday afternoon." Cathy said.

"Alright, I'll see you then." Robert said.

"Okay, bye." The days until Monday seemed to last forever for Cathy, she didn't know what to do with herself, she ran back and forth to the coffee shop and visited with her girlfriends and a couple of boys that she met at the shop. She was kinda touchy about the way people talked to her, she didn't like people to be condescending toward her, but the gang she hung around with were not like that. They would just sit around and talk in general, they didn't look at her any different then they looked at anyone else.

Well, Sunday finally rolled around and Cathy was ready to go and her mom and dad said.

"Would you mind if we come with you?" I'd love that, are you sure?" she asked

"We've stood by you since you were born, why should we stop now?" Del said.

"Thanks you guys." Cathy replied.

"One thing though." Del said.

"I'm paying for the gas, you can't possibly have much left."

"I have enough, but thanks." Cathy said.

So they gassed up and headed for Wellsley. the trip took quite a while cause Cathy was driving the speed limit and no more, Del said.

"You're driving defensively today, is there something wrong?"

"No not really, that accident that Dr. Johnson had kinda scared me somewhat." Cathy said.

"Yeah, it could have been a whole lot worse." Del replied.

"Just thinking about what I would have done if anything had happened to him just gives me the shivers." she said.

"I know what you mean, but that's alright, we've got lots of time." Del said.

When they got to wellsley they went directly to Mr. White's house and the elderly caretaker woman came to the door and said in an Irish brogue.

"Mr. White is sick in bed and I don't think he can get up, he's 82 you know and he hasn't been all that well lately."

"Well, that's alright, we may be able to do this without him, tell him we were here and that we wish him good health." Del aid.

"Thank you sir." the woman answered.

Del went back to the van and told Cathy to drive on back home cause Mr. White was sick in bed and couldn't make it.

"Oh shoot, what are we going to do now?" Cathy asked.

"Cathy, it's not that bad, Dr. Johnson took x rays of his back so maybe he doesn't have to be there." Del said.

"Well, maybe you're right, anyway, I'm hungry, let's go get something to eat." Cathy said.

"Best idea you've had all day." Del said.

By the time they got home, Alice was there and she was sitting in the kitchen with Brenda. Debbie made some coffee and they all sat down and talked about everything that had happened. Alice had tears in her eyes and said.

"I can't believe that my grandfather will finally get recognition for his work."

"I certainly hope he does, It's bigger then you think, look at all the people in wheel chairs, most of them are there because of back problem, all the paraplegics and to say nothing of the quadraplegics, it'll help a lot of people." Cathy said.

Cathy said. "If the A.M.A is not made up of narrow minded old fogy's." Alice said.

"Hey, what do you say we all go out for supper tonight, there's a steak house we've been wanting to try out and I can't think of a better time then tonight." Del said.

"Daddy, you've been spending quite a bit lately and I don't know if you can afford it." Cathy said.

"Listen, when you were working and helping out we had a chance to get ahead a little and now we have a chance to do something for you." Del said.

"Well, if you feel that way about it I'll have two steaks, and Brenda I know can sock away three." Cathy said.

"Yeah right Cathy." Brenda said.

It gave them all the opportunity to visit together for a long period of time and Cathy and Alice were rapidly growing in to a good friendship. And Cathy wanted to have some fun that night because she knew that the following day was going to be a very emotional time for her and very nerve wracking.

If there was ever a time that Cathy needed moral support it was now, Del was taking the day off and every one was planning to go. Alice was a God sent, she had more compassion in her little finger, and understanding, she glowed with it.

They went back home and Brenda said she wanted to watch T.V. for a while and then she was going to bed to rest up for the next day, she had taken the day off too, cause she knew that her sister needed all the help she could get.

Cathy and Alice decided to play a game of rummy and just get to know each other. Del went in to take a shower and Debbie was sewing one of Del's shirts. and Cathy said.

"Ah the home life."

"I like staying home too, I don't care to go to clubs or go out just for the sake of going out." Alice said.

"You're about my age aren't you?" Brenda asked.

"I'm 21." Alice said.

"No offer of marriage yet?" Brenda asked.

"Oh, there was one guy but he loved himself so much there wasn't any room for me." Alice said.

"Gees, That's too bad, but then there are a lot of that kind floating around." Brenda said.

"Yeah, I know, I've had a couple of dates after that but I'm in no hurry, if I go out with a guy and he wants to jump in bed right away I'm gone." Alice said.

"I knew there was a good reason why I liked you right from the start, you're my kind of gal, we think alike, of course, no body would want to jump in bed with me now, with everything dead from the waist down, I wouldn't be interested either."

"I have a feeling we're gonna be friends for a long time."

"I certainly hope so." Cathy said.

"My boss told me that there is an opening at the library right here in Deluth."

"No kidding, are you considering it?"

"I wasn't, but I might when I get back."

"Oh, that would be super."

Cathy and Alice played cards for about an hour and Cathy said.

"It's ten o`clock and we have a rough day tomorrow so we had better get some sleep."

"I think you're right Cathy, I'm tired anyway, we'd better turn in."

The following morning, Cathy woke up early and got everybody up and Debbie said.

"I'm too nervous to cook this morning, we should eat out again."

"We are eating out, and this time it's on me." Cathy said.

"Can you swing it Cathy?" Del said.

"What's it going to cost me daddy, $25.00 dollars, big deal." Cathy said. "Yeah, I suppose so." Del answered.

"Plus, I don't want mom to cook this morning, let's try to be at the restaurant for eight thirty and we'll have time to eat before we go." Cathy said.

"Sounds good to me, let's do it." Del said.

So off they went to the restaurant

Dr. Johnson came in about nine and everybody was there except Mr. White and he said. "Where's Robert?"

"He was sick in bed when we got there, and the lady that was taking care of him said he couldn't get out of bed, so we took a chance on going there without him since you have some x-rays of him already." Cathy said.

"Well, we don't have much of a choice do we?" Al said.

"No, not much that I could see." Del said.

Al said. "Well, we'll present what we have and hope it will suffice."

Dr. Johnson sat down to eat and after that they went to the A.M.A office where there were seven Doctors waiting to hear this claim. The only ones they wanted in the inner office was Dr. Johnson, alone at first and then they would call people as they needed them. Dr. Johnson had his arms full of papers, x rays, documents of all sorts. He went in and didn't come out for an hour and a half. Finally, he came out with another man and they asked for Alice Bains, so she got up and went in. Alice was in there till lunch time, cause they started to come out of the office at 11:55 and said they were breaking for lunch.

Cathy was on pins and needles wondering what was going on, Dr. Johnson came out, and then Alice, and Cathy said.

"What is happening?" "Let's go to lunch and we'll talk about it." Dr. Johnson said. So again, Cathy was filled with anxiety and she feared the worse. When they got to the restaurant she was bouncing like a rubber ball, and she said.

"Someone talk to me before I blow up."

Dr. Johnson was in no hurry, he got his lunch and came over to the table, meanwhile, Del was getting food for his gang and again Cathy said. "Well?"

"Dr. Johnson will tell you." Alice said.

"All I can tell you at this point Cathy is that the Doctors are knee deep in the procedural records, which is very promising." Dr. Johnson said.

Cathy let out a big sigh of relief and said.

"My God, don't do that to me."

"Sorry Cathy, but at the A.M.A. it's not wise to discuss a case out in the halls." Al said. "I didn't know that." Cathy replied.

"I know, and I should have told you but it slipped my mind." "So, what's gonna happen now?" Cathy asked.

"They have to completely review the records before they make a decision." Al said. "And how long is that going to take?" Cathy asked.

"Relax Cathy, first of all, the Doctors that are in the A.M.A. now in this day and age are more open minded and can vision the future better then the Doctors back in Doctor Franklin's day, and, they never heard of Dr. James Franklin." Al said.

"I suppose it will take them time to soak all this in." Cathy said.

"Yes it will, but I will tell you one thing, their thinking is positive." Al said.

"Thank you, I've waited this long I guess I can wait a little longer." Cathy said.

"Well Cathy, sometimes the wheels of progress turn very slowly." Al said. "I've got a set that's anything but." Cathy replied.

"I'll bet you could too." Al said. everybody laughed.

After lunch they all went back to the A.M.A. office and waited for the Doctors to get back from lunch, and they were in the habit of taking long ones. After a few minutes one of them came up the stairs like he had eaten too much and said.

"Everybody ready?" "Yes sir." Cathy said.

Then another came, and then another, all in all Cathy counted six of them, after the sixth one got there, Dr. Johnson went in and Alice too. Then Dr. Johnson came back out and asked Cathy to come in, he said.

"They are ready for you Cathy."

Cathy went in with Del and Debbie and there in front of her was a judge's bench only it seated six people, It looked like the court of courts and Cathy thought how scary it all looked, all those men sitting there in their black robes like if you disagree with them they yell, off with her head. One of them spoke and said. "What is your name?" "Cathy Woods sir."

"I hear a lot of good things about you, you've been a busy girl." "Yes sir, I suppose I have."

"We've been checking Mr. White's x rays and looking over the procedural records and this is what we have decided to do."

"We feel at this time that if all procedures are followed to the letter that Dr. Johnson can operate on you any time you are ready, but you have to take all responsibilities." the man said.

Cathy at that point collapsed in her chair, Dr. Johnson went over to her aid and was rubbing her hand and talking to her.

Finally she came around and said.

"You're not joking are you?"

"No miss, we are very serious." the man said.

"In that case, I want all of you to file past me here so I can give you all a great big kiss." Cathy said.

Dr. Johnson noticed that she was still reeling and he stayed by her through the whole thing, not moving from her chair.

"Cathy, you don't look well, I think you should go outside and get some fresh air." Al said.

"Yeah, maybe so." she said.

"Gentlemen, may we be excused, Cathy needs some air, the news was too much for her." Dr. Johnson said.

"Certainly Dr., I would like a meeting with you before we proceed with the operation though." The head Dr. said.

"That's fine, have your office call mine and set it up." Al said.

"Okay, we'll see you." the other Dr. said.

Del started pushing Cathy out of the big room and before he could get to the door, Cathy burst out crying. Debbie said.

"What's the matter with her, I've never seen her like this before?"

"Realization." Dr. Johnson said.

"What do you mean?" Del said.

"She's just now realizing what the Dr.'s said, she'll be fine." Al said.

Cathy's crying changed from shock to frantic to sobbing. Debbie said.

"Are you okay honey?" Debbie asked.

"Oh mom, did you hear what they said?" Cathy cried.

"Yes, isn't that wonderful?" Debbie said.

"I can't explain the feeling, I worked so hard to get there and when I did I couldn't handle it." Cathy said.

"I know you worked hard, and you deserve this operation." Debbie replied.

"Thanks mom, and daddy, thank you, and thank you to everyone who had a hand in this, I love you all." Cathy said.

"Me too?" Alice said.

"Especially you, if it wasn't for the fact that you kept all your grandfather's records, this would never have happened." Cathy said.

"We're forgetting one, excuse me." Cathy said.

Cathy took her phone and called Mr. White to tell him the good news, and she said.

"Hello, may I speak with Mr. White please, What, oh no, I'm so sorry, yes, we will be there." and she hung up.

"What's the matter Cathy, you're pale as a ghost?" Del asked.

Her lip started to tremble and she began to cry and said.

"Mr. White passed away about twenty minutes ago."

"Oh my god, Del said, You received your news about twenty minutes ago."

"I know, It's as if it was providence, he hung on until he knew I was gonna be okay." Cathy cried.

"You don't believe that do you Cathy?" Del asked.

"Oh yes I do, look where my beliefs have gotten me." Cathy said.

"I suppose, if you want something bad enough." Dr. Johnson said.

Chapter 14

"And I did, but not at his expense." Cathy said.

"I'm sure it wasn't that way at all honey. Del said. What do you say we all go home, it's been a trying day and Cathy is very tired."

"Sounds good, we'll see you later Dr.." Debbie said.

So Cathy, Del, Debbie, and Alice all got in the van and drove back home, and when they got there Alice said.

"I have to be going too cause I have to work tomorrow."

"Aw, do you have to." Cathy asked.

"Yes, I'm afraid so, but I can't thank you enough for what you have done for my grandfather and for me." Alice said.

"I will tell you this though, Cathy said, if we rewrite medical history, the name James Franklin will be there."

Now Alice started to cry, she threw her arms around Cathy and said.

"God bless you." Alice said.

"You may think I'm crazy, but do you know what I think?" Cathy said.

"No, what." Alice said.

"I think I was meant to get stabbed in the back in order to bring all this about, what do you think of that?" Cathy said.

"Do you think it's possible?" Alice asked.

"Well, if it is, God won't let me down, he hasn't so far." Cathy said.

"Yes I know, and if he is handling it, worry pas."

At the funeral for Mr. White, Cathy and Alice cried like he was a close relative, cause he was the last known person that Dr. Franklin had operated on. About one week went by and Dr. Johnson called and said he wanted to see Cathy in his office so they could set a date to do the operation. First thing the next morning Cathy drove down town and stopped at the coffee shop, and she ran in to Bobby, he was sitting at a table with some of Cathy's friends and Cathy went and sat elsewhere. One of the girls came over and said.

"How come you didn't sit with us Cathy?"

"Because of Bobby." she said.

"What's the matter with him." she asked.

"He doesn't want anything to do with me cause I'm in a wheel chair." she told her.

"You're kidding, he never gave me the impression that he was that way." she said.

"Well, he is, and if you guys don't mind, I'd rather not sit where he is." Cathy replied.

"I don't blame you." she said.

And the girl left and went back to her table, just long enough to pick up her stuff and she came back to sit with Cathy.

Then another and another, until Bobby was sitting alone.

He Caught the gist of what was going on and he got up and came over to the table, and he said.

"You don't have to treat me, like I have Leprosy Cathy."

"Listen, Bobby, get lost or else." Cathy said.

"Or else what." he said.

"Or else, I'm gonna come in here one of these days and get out of this chair and clean your clock." Cathy said.

The girls asked, are you going for an operation?"

"I'm going to Dr. Johnson's office now and we will set a date for it." Cathy said.

Those girls started to squeal they were so happy for her.

Bobby, who was still standing there said.

"Good luck."

"I don't need luck, I have the Lord on my side." Cathy said.

Bobby walked away feeling sad for the situation he was in that he had created for himself.

The girls all sat around talking about what had transpired and how soon she would know, and Cathy said.

"I'm going to see the Dr. now and I'll know as soon as I come out of there."

She left the restaurant and drove off towards the Dr.'s office. When she got there she was allowed to go in right away and when the Dr. came in to the examination room he said.

"Hi there tiger, how's it going?"

"Fine I guess." Cathy said.

"Now, when could you be ready to go in for this operation?" Al asked.

"Any time, I don't have to take time off from my work." Cathy replied.

"Ha, Yeah right Cathy." Dr. Johnson said.

"Now, what is this operation gonna cost me?" Cathy asked.

"Well, I spoke to the A.M.A. and since it is a first time thing, and it could work or not work, they feel that they don't want to charge you anything, and I don't want to charge you either." Al said.

"Hey, you can't beat that with a stick." Cathy replied.

"Now, understand, that we can only go in once, if it doesn't work, that's it, but I've been studying the records and the x rays from Mr. White and learning the procedure, according to what I see there, it's not hard." Al said.

"Well, I'm ready any time Doc. the ball is in your court." Cathy said.

"Okay, I'll call the hospital and reserve a room, oh and after the operation, you have to lay on your back for one month, the A.M.A. is picking up the tab on the hospital cost, and everything has to be done from that bed and that position, everything." Al said. as he showed her a picture from Dr. Franklin's files.

"Piece of cake Doc., If I can go through what I have been through I can do that standing on my head." Cathy said.

"Don't be too sure of yourself, you will be very stiff at the end of all this, and then you have to go through extensive therapy." Al said.

"I know what I'm facing Dr. but do you know any other way that will allow me to walk again?" Cathy asked.

"Unfortunately no." Al said.

"There you go." Cathy replied.

"Well, your courage brought you this far." Al said.

"Dr. If you do your thing and the hospital does their thing, I will do mine." Cathy said.

"Very good, just so you understand." Al said.

"I understand that there is a man in a wheel chair because he didn't listen to his Doctor, I will not let that happen to me." Cathy said.

"Good girl, now, how about I give you a call when I get news from the hospital?" Al said.

"Fine Doc. I'll wait for your call." Cathy said.

She drove back home and the mental anxiety made her very tired and she went in her room and laid down for a while, she had no more to do for the rest of the day so she might as well relax she thought, the operation was gonna take a lot out of her so she had better get all the rest she could get.

Debbie was talking to Brenda on the phone at her place of employment and she was telling her about Cathy's visit with Dr. Johnson that morning and Cathy hadn't discussed it with her as yet, but she figured that she would do it at supper time when everyone is there. As she was talking she was interrupted by a beep and she told Brenda to hold the line and she went to the other call, it was Dr. Johnson and he wanted to talk to Cathy, but Debbie told him that she was sleeping and could she take a message. But Cathy yelled from the bedroom and said.

"I'm not sleeping mom."

"Dr. Johnson, could you hold for a minute?" Debbie said.

"Sure." he said.

"Brenda, I have to let you go, It's for Cathy, okay?" Debbie said.

Debbie picked up the cordless and went in to Cathy's room and said."

"Hold on Dr. here she is."

"Hello." Cathy called out.

"Cathy, Dr. Johnson here, I got you a room for one week from today, and they want you there for 8:00 A.M. for preparation, cause we go in at 9:00". Al said.

"Fine, I'll be there, MMM, okay, bye." Cathy replied.

Debbie who was standing by said.

"What was that all about honey?"

"I go in for my operation one week from today." Cathy said.

"Oh my God, that soon?" Debbie cried.

"Can't be soon enough for me." Cathy replied.

When her dad and sister got home from work she was still sleeping and Del asked.

"How come?" and Debbie said

"I'll let her tell you that at supper, so wash up it's almost ready."

A few minutes later Debbie said.

"Supper is ready, Brenda, go wake up your sister will you please?"

"Sure." Brenda replied.

They all sat down at the table and after Cathy had taken some food Del said.

"How was your day today Cathy?"

"Fine, I got an appointment." Cathy said.

"For what?" Del asked.

"For my operation." Cathy replied.

"You're kidding, when?" Del said.

"One week from today." Cathy told him.

"Holy smokes, that was fast." he said.

"Yes, and you can relax, cause the A.M.A. is paying for the whole thing." Cathy said.

"What, why are they doing that?" Del asked.

"Cause It's a first and it could go either way, I have to sign a paper absolving them of all responsibility." Cathy said.

"Are you going to do that?" Del asked.

"Oh yes." Cathy said.

"What if it doesn't work?" Del asked again.

"Oh ye of little faith." she said.

"Yeah, I should know better then to say something like that in front of you." Del said.

"If the Dr. does his job, I'll do mine, I have to lay perfectly still on my back for one month, and I don't intend on going back in this chair." Cathy said.

"You've got more courage then any body I've ever known, if anybody deserves to walk again it's you." Del said.

"Good Lord daddy, you'd do the same thing." Cathy said.

"I'm not too sure about that, there are a lot of people in wheel chairs that have just accepted the way things are, but not you, you fought hard for what you have done." Del said.

"I am my father's daughter, and you're a fighter, I've seen you work two jobs just so your family would not have to do without." Cathy said.

"Well, that's different." Del said.

"No it's not daddy, now you're taking credit away from yourself." Cathy replied.

"All I'm saying is that I've seen you stumble and fall and you get up and attack the problem with as much enthusiasm as before." Del said.

"What can I say, I take after you and mom." Cathy said.

For the next week, Cathy didn't go far, she hung around the house and slept a lot preparing herself for the big operation she must face. A couple of days before she was to go in the hospital she got a phone call from some lawyer telling her that Mr. Robert White had passed away and that he had left Cathy some money and could she please come to his office at her earliest convenience.

The following day Del took the day off and drove his daughter over to Wellsley to see this attorney, when they got there they found that it was on the second floor and there was no elevator, so Del said.

"Wait here and I'll go up and see him."

So Del went up the long flight of stairs and found the office, On the door was the name "Brent Nini Attorney" and Del walked in. At a reception desk was a cute little girl, she looked up and said "yes, can I help you."

"I'm Del Woods, Cathy Woods's father."

"Yes," she said.

"My daughter received a phone call from the Attorney in this office and he said he wanted to see her." Del told her.

"Where is she now?" she asked.

"Down stairs, she can't come up, she's in a wheel chair and there is no elevator." Del said.

"Oh, I'll let my father know you're here." she said.

This man came out and said.

"I'm Brent Nini, can I help you?"

"Yes, my daughter received a phone call from you stating that you wanted to see her and she is waiting down stairs cause she is in a wheel chair and there is no elevator." Del told him.

"Oh yes, Cathy Woods." he said surprised.

"I can't leave my daughter unattended down stairs so I don't know what you want to do but we'll be down there." Del said.

Del walked out and went back downstairs and said.

"Sorry it took so long honey, you okay?"

"Other then people staring at me, yeah, I'm fine." Cathy said.

Del sat at the foot of the steps and they were talking when he heard the lawyer coming, he came down the steps and said.

"Are you Cathy Woods?" he asked.

"Yes sir I am." Cathy said.

"Do you have some Identification?" he asked.

"Yes, what's this about anyway?" Cathy asked.

"You don't know?" he asked.

"No sir, I don't, I know that you said something about Mr. White but that is all I know." Cathy said.

"Well, Mr. Robert White left you a considerable amount of money when he died and he told me the morning he passed away that it was for your operation and convalescence, to help see you through, you see, Robert had no surviving relatives, and he wanted to help you before he died but he didn't have time so when he started to feel real bad he got scared and called me so I could do it for him." He said.

"My God, what a sweet man." Cathy said.

"You'll think sweeter then that when you see this check, sign right here miss and I'll go back upstairs and make some copies so you will have some records and I'll give you some money." Brent said.

So Cathy signed the papers and he took off up the stairs.

He came back a few minutes later and said.

"These stairs are gonna kill me, okay, here are your copies and here is your check for $52,964.72 and other then my fee, that is all he had in the bank, the house he gave to the woman that was taking care of him." He said.

"Oh my Lord daddy, why did he do that?" Cathy asked. The attorney said.

"He told me that he was doing it because he loved you, cause I asked him the same question." he said.

"She has that effect on people." Del said.

"Oh daddy." Cathy sobbing.

"My daughter is going through a big operation in two days and I had better get her home so she can get some rest, so thank you very much and I wish Robert was here so I could thank him too." Del said.

"I'm sure he heard you daddy." Cathy said.

"Well, thanks again, come on babe, let's go." Del said.

Del pushed Cathy's chair out the door and loaded her in the front seat of the car, and placed the chair in the trunk and drove off. Cathy looked at her father like she was totally confused and she said.

"Dad, find a coffee shop some where cause I need to relax and figure out what just happened." she laughed.

"Okay honey, my head is spinning too." Del said.

"Daddy, is this check real?" Cathy asked.

"It looks real to me." Del said.

Chapter 15

"This can't be happening, almost fifty three thousand dollars dropped in my lap, I've never seen that kind of money." Cathy said.

"Neither have I." Del said.

"We have to talk to mom of course but I want to deposit this money in your account." Cathy said.

"Why?" Del asked.

"To help you pay for all the things you did for me, and anyway, that's why Mr. White gave me the money in the first place." Cathy said.

When they got home and told Debbie, she almost fainted, Brenda said.

"I want some."

After everybody soaked it all in they were making plans on how they could spend it and Cathy said.

"I'm putting the money in dad's account, so talk to him." Cathy told her.

"I can't spend that money Brenda, it belongs to Cathy." Del said.

"Cute you guys, very cute." Brenda replied.

Well, the big day rolled around and they all went with Cathy to the hospital and checked her in, the Interns came and picked up Cathy and placed her on one of those cots on wheels and rolled her away. Debbie was crying and so was Brenda,

Del's bottom lip wasn't too steady either, Dr. Johnson came around the corner and said.

"Hey you people, buck up, listen, the worse that could happen is she will leave here in that again." and he pointed to the wheel chair."

"That's not too encouraging Doc.." Debbie said.

"I have every confidence that Cathy will walk out of here." Al said.

"I certainly hope you're right. Del said. But it still hurts to see her go in there."

"I know Del, but she'll be alright, I'll let you know when it's over." Al said.

"Oh, we'll be right here." Del told him.

"In that case, come up to the third floor with me and you can wait in the Doctor's lounge, it's much more comfortable." Al said.

"Thank you very much." Del thanked him. and the Dr. was gone.

The operation, a first time procedure took seven hours, and finally Dr. Johnson came out and sat down with them and said.

"Man, I'm bushed."

"How did it go?" Del asked.

"Well, once you get used to the procedure it shouldn't take that long but I think I have fused all the tendons and other things that have long words that the records called for, I wanted to go in once and only once, now it's up to God and Cathy." he said.

The following month was very hard on everybody, especially Cathy, she had to just lay there and go through the embarrassment of having some one help her go to the bath room, she couldn't have any hard foods that would make her have to push to go, in other words she couldn't move those back muscles at all for one month.

They couldn't move her to change the sheets or her gown or anything, after about three weeks of her lying there, Dr. Johnson came in and said.

"Hey, how's my favorite patient?"

"Don't get too close unless you have a gas mask Doc." Cathy said.

"Cathy, If you can walk out of here, we're not gonna worry about a little thing like that." the Dr. Said.

"It's your nose." she said.

Now Cathy, I'm going to perform a little test on you and I will tell you what I am going to do and you don't move a muscle, even if you feel something, you got that?" the Dr. Said.

"Yes." Cathy answered.

"Now, I'm going to touch your foot with a needle like a scratch, okay? and I want you to tell me if you feel anything." he said.

"Okay." she said.

He started to scrape the bottom of her foot with the needle and a tear appeared in one of her eyes and he said.

"You felt that, didn't you?"

"If you don't stop hurting me I'm gonna kick you." she said.

Now, Dr, Johnson had a tear in his eye and he said.

"By George, I think we did something Cathy."

"Yeah, you fixed it so I couldn't chase you around the block." she said.

"Another week and you have to learn how to walk all over again Cathy." he said.

"Listen, if I can put up with this smell I can do anything." Cathy replied.

"I suppose in time we will have to develop new ways of doing this but for now I have to follow the script to the letter." the Dr. Said.

"I understand, now do me a favor and get lost, this is very embarrassing." Cathy said.

"Okay my little chickadee." he said laughing.

"Don't make me laugh, Dr's orders." Cathy said.

Another week went by and by this time they had to bring in some Deodorizers and all sorts of stuff to try to squelch the stench. Dr. Johnson came in wearing a gas mask and Cathy couldn't help but laugh out loud, and he said as he took off the mask.

"Whew, you need a bath."

Now she was laughing real hard. He said, "come on get out of bed you lazy thing."

"Am I getting up today?" she asked.

"If you lay there one more day you're gonna rot." he said.

The orderly's came in and Dr. Johnson said.

"Gentlemen, very gentle, she hasn't moved in one month, so we don't want to break her."

"Now Cathy, do you feel anything in your back, like pain or discomfort?" he asked.

"No, but then I haven't tried to move yet." she said.

The orderly's took her very gently and rolled her on her side and slid the sheets out from under her and she said.

"Oh my God, I've never felt anything that felt so good."

"You mean getting rid of the dirty sheets?" he asked.

"Listen you, if I can walk, you're in trouble." she said.

Two nurses came in and said it was time for her bath and the Dr. said.

"Well, I'll see you later." he said and left.

By the time Del and Debbie came in that morning she was laying on her back and all clean and she smelled like roses. Del said.

"This is the most beautiful sight I have ever seen."

Dr. Johnson came in and said.

"We have to test you again missy, tell me if you feel this?"

He scraped that pin across her foot. she said.

"If you don't stop sticking me with that needle I'll."

"You'll what, you can't walk remember." he said.

"That's what you think, if I can move one toe can I walk." she asked.

"Yeah, but you can't." he said.

Del took the Dr. aside and said.

"Why are you trying to discourage her?"

"I'm not, it's part of the therapy." he said.

"Watch this weisenheimer." she said.

"I'm waiting." the Dr. said.

"I'm trying." she said.

All at once she moved her big toe such a slight amount and the Dr. said.

"I'm getting out of here, she threatened to kick me."

"Dear Lord, I can move my toe, and I can feel it." she said.

Debbie was crying and so was Del. They had never seen or felt anything so wonderful in their lives. Dr. Johnson said.

"Now Cathy, I want you to lay around like this for two days, you can move around if you can or want to, if you feel you want to sit up call the nurse and she will get you some help, you can also sit in a wheel chair for a while, roll down to the cafeteria and have a coffee, but under no circumstances try to walk, okay?"

"Okay captain, aye aye sir."

"Still a wise guy huh." he said.

Cathy's legs were uncovered and Debbie put her hand on Cathy's leg and Cathy said.

"Oooo your hand is cold."

"My God, you felt that?" Debbie asked.

"Yes I did mom." Cathy said.

"That's fantastic sweetheart." Debbie said.

Dr. Johnson came back in and Debbie told him about Cathy feeling her hand and he said.

"Great, now Cathy, the therapy fellas will be here in a minute and I want to introduce you to them and tell them a few things about you." he said.

Two guys came in to the room and he said.

"These are the fellows I told you about, they will put you through therapy, and I want to tell them in front of you so that everyone will understand." he said.

He spoke to the two standing there and he said.

"What I want you to do is put one hand under her knee and the other on her foot and lift one foot, that is twelve inches high, do that slowly four times the first day, then I want the same procedure four times tomorrow." and he went on explaining how he wanted it done. Cathy went through bed therapy for four days until she could move her legs by herself, then the Dr. told her that she was ready to start walking. That morning they took her into a big room and there were two nurses waiting for her.

They locked the door and undressed her and placed her in a whirlpool bath that one nurse said would soften her muscles.

After that, they opened the door and started to work with her to get her to stand up, it was a very slow process, her muscles were very stiff but one nurse assured her that in time they would loosen up. She didn't make much progress the first day but it felt good just feeling the floor with her feet.

It went on that way for another month and then she was ready to go home. Dr. Johnson came in her room and said.

"I hear you are leaving us today?"

"Yes oh great one." Cathy said.

"I've got your great one, stand up and turn around, now stand with both your feet flat on the floor and lift up your shirt Hmmm, you've got a nice looking back."

"Okay Smarty, did you see enough?" she asked.

"Yeah okay you can put your shirt down, these young people, such a pain." he said.

"On a more serious note, I want to thank you for everything you have done." Cathy said.

"You did it Cathy, I just operated, and before you go there are some people I would want you to meet." he said.

"Okay, lets go." she said.

They started walking down the hallway, not fast, but walking.

He took her to a big room where there were at least seven wheel chairs and he said.

"Ladies and gentlemen, this is Cathy Woods A paraplegic, and what she has done, you can do, she came in here in a wheel chair and she will walk out. I'm Dr. Johnson and I can help you."

They all wanted to talk to Cathy to find out more about it, after that, they walked back to Cathy's room where her mom and dad were waiting and Brenda came running up the stairs and over to her sister's room, and she said.

"Dear God, It's good to see you on your feet again."

"Come on I'll race you down the hallway." Cathy said.

"Very funny you two, Del said. What do you say we go home." That's when a reporter from the Deluth news came over to talk to Cathy, and Del said.

"We're going home now, but you can stop by anytime to talk to her, right now she's tired and has been through enough." Del said. "Yes sir." he said.

They rolled Cathy out in a wheel chair as far as the door which is standard procedure and then she stood up and walked to the car. Cathy said.

"Daddy, is my chair in the trunk?" "Yeah, why?"

"Cause I want you to stop at the coffee shop and let me go in to see my girl friends, I want to surprise them."

"Okay honey, you deserve the glory." Del said.

When they got there, Del went through the routine and placed her in her chair and she wheeled in to the shop. The girls all greeted her very warmly and she said.

"Hey you guys, can I sit in that empty seat there."

"Sure, one of them said, let me give you a hand."

"Never mind, I'll just walk over."

When she got up and walked over to the seat you could hear those girls scream two blocks down the road. She stayed about fifteen minutes and said she had to go cause her family was waiting for her in the car. She walked behind her chair pushing it very slowly like the Dr. had told her to do and who was walking in but Bobby. Cathy said.

"Hi Bobby." and kept on walking. He just stood there with his mouth hanging open. She went back to the car and said to her folks.

"Now I feel good, let's go home."

"How would you like it if I have your van changed back to normal so you could drive it.?"

"Oh, I'd love that daddy, I love that van and it would be a constant reminder for me what the Lord did for me." she said.

"I figured you would, I'll get at it right away." del said.

The next day some reporters came over to talk to the family and get the facts about all that had happened.

The following Monday the paper boy flung the paper on the front porch and Cathy went out to get it and when she opened it, there on the front page was Cathy's picture and the whole story about what had happened, and the head lines that read, OLD FASHIONED COURAGE.

CATHY WOODS BLESSED

THE END
STORY BY VINCE ALBERTS.

Printed in the United States
By Bookmasters